Jameson knew

close to

She was as beautifu

her ten years before. Actually, even more so, because now she was a woman who had experienced life and hadn't been marred by its harsh realities.

Until now.

He lounged back in his chair, a vision of Cassie forming in his mind. Red shoulder-length hair, bright emerald-green eyes a man could get lost in. He scrubbed his hands down his face and shot to his feet.

How could he think of Cassie in that way? He had no right.

* * *

REUNION REVELATIONS: Secrets surface when old friends—and foes—get together.

Hidden in the Wall–Valerie Hansen (LIS#84) January 2008
Missing Persons–Shirlee McCoy (LIS#88) February 2008
Don't Look Back–Margaret Daley (LIS#92) March 2008
In His Sights–Carol Steward (LIS#96) April 2008
A Face in the Shadows–Lenora Worth (LIS#100) May 2008
Final Justice–Marta Perry (LIS#104) June 2008

Books by Margaret Daley

Love Inspired Suspense

Hearts on the Line #23
Heart of the Amazon #37
So Dark the Night #43
Vanished #51
Buried Secrets #72
Don't Look Back #92

Love Inspired

The Power of Love #168
Family for Keeps #183
Sadie's Hero #191
The Courage To Dream #205
What the Heart Knows #236
A Family for Tory #245
**Gold in the Fire* #273
**A Mother for Cindy* #283
**Light in the Storm* #297
The Cinderella Plan #320
**When Dreams Come True* #339
**Tidings of Joy* #369
***Once Upon a Family* #393
***Heart of the Family* #425

*The Ladies of Sweetwater Lake
**Fostered by Love

MARGARET DALEY

feels she has been blessed. She has been married over thirty years to her husband, Mike, whom she met in college. He is a terrific support and her best friend. They have one son, Shaun. Margaret has been writing for many years and loves to tell a story. When she was a little girl, she would play with her dolls and make up stories about their lives. Now she writes these stories down. She especially enjoys weaving stories about families and how faith in God can sustain a person when things get tough. When she isn't writing, she is fortunate to be a teacher for students with special needs. Margaret has taught for over twenty years and loves working with her students. She has also been a Special Olympics coach and has participated in many sports with her students.

Don't Look Back

MARGARET DALEY

Published by Steeple Hill Books™

Special thanks and acknowledgment are given to Margaret Daley for her contribution to the REUNION REVELATIONS miniseries.

STEEPLE HILL BOOKS

ISBN-13: 978-0-373-44282-9
ISBN-10: 0-373-44282-3

DON'T LOOK BACK

This edition published by arrangement with Steeple Hill Books.

www.SteepleHill.com

Printed in U.S.A.

But if we walk in the light, as he is in the light, we have fellowship one with another, and the blood of Jesus Christ his Son cleanseth us from all sin.

—*I John* 1:7

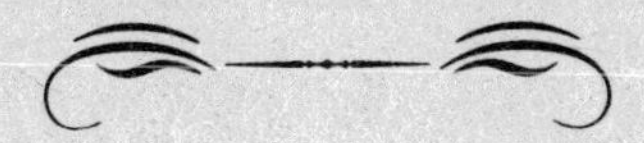

To the other authors who worked with me on this continuity: Valerie Hansen, Shirlee McCoy, Carol Steward, Lenora Worth and Marta Perry.

You all are the best!

PROLOGUE

"I didn't want it to come to this, but you just couldn't stop snooping. You forced me to do this." The intruder approached the figure sprawled on the floor, nudged him, then bent down and felt for a pulse.

With the job finished, the killer scanned the room to make sure nothing was left behind before walking to the door and slipping outside. On the steps he placed a call and said, "It's done. He won't be a problem anymore."

"Good. We can't afford for this to get out. We'd be ruined. Did he tell anyone about what he'd discovered?"

For a few seconds the killer fumbled for an answer. "I think I got here in time. I have his computer and recorder."

"You *think* you got there in time?"

"I'll make sure I did."

"I don't have to tell you what will happen if you don't." The connection went dead.

ONE

Two months earlier

Cassie Winters spied him across the Event Hall at the Mossy Oak Inn where the dinner and fund-raiser for the library expansion was being held. Her heartbeat increased at the sight of him, just as it had when she'd been in his journalism class ten years ago. But instead of his usual jeans, blazer and tie, he was dressed in a black tuxedo. She'd never seen him in formal attire, but Dr. Jameson King had changed little over time. His dark brown hair still looked tousled, and his tall, muscular build was still on the lean side.

"Cassie, are you listening?" Her friend Jennifer Pappas moved into Cassie's line of vision. "Have you heard anything about the skeleton they found under the library sidewalk?"

"Who hasn't? Everyone has been talking about it." Cassie shivered.

Kate Brooks, another friend, sidled closer and lowered her voice. "I hate to think what happened to the woman. Do you think it was someone who attended Magnolia College?"

"I hope not. But there were some women who didn't come to the reunion in June, who haven't been heard from in years." Suddenly cold, Cassie shuddered and hugged herself. "To think a murder happened ten years ago, not too far from here." *Murder on their quiet campus.* The very thought unnerved her.

"To someone we may have known," Jennifer added in her usual quiet voice.

Cassie scanned the crowd again, hoping to get another glimpse of Jameson King. Quinn Nelson, the assistant basketball coach, and Edgar Ortiz, the assistant director of Admissions, had joined him and Dr. Cornell Rutherford, the head of the English Department. The coach patted Jameson on the back, then laughed at something Dr. Rutherford said.

Cassie started to look away when Jameson turned his head, and her gaze connected with his cobalt-blue eyes. For a few seconds, she experienced all over again the lure those eyes had for her.

He smiled at her. Heat scored her cheeks at being caught staring at him. He said something to Dr. Rutherford, then weaved his way through the crowd toward her.

"Excuse me," Cassie said to her two friends who were still discussing the recently found skeleton. "I see someone I haven't had a chance to talk to yet."

Kate laughed. "I see who's heading this way. Although you didn't major in journalism, I do believe he was your favorite teacher."

"He was a lot of students' favorite teacher." Cassie brushed her hair behind her ears, a nervous habit she wished she could break.

"He still is. His classes are always full from what I hear." Jennifer took a sip of her punch.

Cassie walked toward him before he had a chance to join the three of them. All she needed was an audience when she finally talked to him after all these years. She wondered what else he had been doing besides teaching. Her brother had kept her informed some since Jameson had been Scott's college adviser, but she'd dared not ask her brother too many questions or she would have never heard the end of it. It was bad enough her friends kidded her about her college crush on her professor.

Jameson stopped in front of her. "Cassie, it's so good to see you again."

The other people crowded into the room faded away. Cassie offered a smile, clenching a glass of punch in her hand. "It's good to see you, too. I wanted to tell you how sorry I was to hear about your wife's death last year."

One of his dark eyebrows rose. "You knew? It wasn't common knowledge in Magnolia Falls."

"As you know, Scott works for the Savannah paper, and he told me." She remembered her surprise when her younger brother had called her about the news. Although Jameson had always worn a wedding ring, there had never been any evidence of a wife. All the students had speculated about the mysterious woman whom no one had ever seen. Some people had even wondered if a wife had really existed.

"How's Scott doing? I haven't talked to him lately."

Suddenly she wanted to share her good news with someone who would care. She glanced around her, the press of people making a private conversation impossible. "I could use some fresh air. Care to join me for a walk?"

For a brief moment surprise widened his eyes before he said, "Sure."

Cassie put her glass cup on a nearby table, then led the way toward the entrance. After Jameson opened the door for her, she stepped outside into the warm August evening, but the large live oaks dripping with Spanish moss offered a cool, private canopy over the stone path. She paused near some gardenia bushes. Their sweet, heavy fragrance laced the light breeze.

"Is something wrong with Scott?" Jameson came to her side, his expression etched with worry.

"Oh, no. I didn't want to say anything inside, but I know you're aware of Scott's drinking problem. He has been sober for the past year. We went out to dinner the other night to celebrate his success."

A smile lit Jameson's face. "That's wonderful news."

"He owes you so much. Getting the job at the newspaper really helped him turn his life around after the accident. He wouldn't have gotten it if you hadn't contacted your friend there."

"Scott landed the job on his own merit. I just gave him a reference. Your brother's work was, is, excellent, and since he couldn't play pro ball, what better job for him since he majored in journalism."

Cassie glimpsed a stone bench nearby. "Do you want to sit?"

"No, let's walk some. I've been sitting at the computer way too much lately."

"I didn't realize you held that many office hours."

He started forward. "I'm working on a novel. I recently sold one."

"Congratulations." Cassie fell into step next to him on the path that led to the back of the inn. The sun brushed the tops of a line of pine trees on the west side of the property.

"Thanks. Since my wife's death, I've had more time on my hands, and it was something I've always wanted to do."

"Is this your first book?"

Jameson headed toward the small pond behind the inn. "Yes, well, my first work of fiction. I've written several academic books over the years."

"Ah, yes. I remember you discussing one of them in class."

"That was a long time ago."

His voice sounded tired and matched a world-weary look in his eyes, prompting Cassie to peer at him as she stopped at the edge of the pond. "Twelve years. I was a sophomore the first time I took one of your classes. I believe that was your first year at the school."

The blue of his eyes darkened, revealing a hint of vulnerability in his expression. He shifted away from her and stared at the ducks swimming in the water. A subtle tension hummed in the air.

"Dr. King?"

He blinked and focused on her face. "Sorry. I was just thinking about the past. And please call me Jameson. We're no longer teacher and student."

Weariness coated each of his words. She had a strong urge to comfort him but didn't know how. He had always been such a private person.

Determined to interject some lightness into the conversation, Cassie said, "I was surprised you were here this evening. I've been back several times for functions at the college, but you've always been in hiding." She would know because she'd always looked for him. "I guess now I know you've been madly composing the next American bestseller. Hemingway and Faulkner will have to move over for you."

He chuckled, the dullness in his gaze vanishing. "Hardly. It's a murder mystery. I hope a quick, entertaining read, but not a book anyone would proclaim a literary masterpiece. The truth is, I don't usually come to many events at the college."

"What made you this time?"

He looked long and deep into her eyes, his head tilted to the side. "You know, I'm not sure. I hadn't planned on it this morning, but I sold my book and wanted to celebrate. This seemed like as good a place as any." The corners of his mouth formed a grin. "I've seen quite a few former students at this fund-raiser. I have fond memories of your graduating class. Some of my best students were in it."

Her pulse quickened. His gaze seared straight into her heart. "So our class was better than my brother's?"

He laughed. "You can't draw me into a family rivalry. I plead the Fifth."

His husky laughter wrapped around her, its sound wonderful to hear. She suspected he hadn't laughed much lately, since his wife's death. She fixed an impish smile on her face and widened her eyes in mock innocence. "Oh, I'd never do that to my baby brother."

"Yeah, sure. I have an older sister. I know a few things about sibling rivalry."

That was one of the few personal pieces of information she knew about him. He had always been an enigma, which was what probably drew her to him. She loved to solve puzzles—in fact, did the crossword in the newspaper every morning before starting her day. "Interesting.

An older sister. Any other deep, dark secrets you want to share?"

Secrets? Jameson scrambled to keep his countenance neutral. For a brief time he'd forgotten. Cassie had that effect on him.

He turned away, staring at two ducks herding their babies up the slope on the other side of the pond. "Don't we all have secrets?"

"I'm an open book." She waggled her finger at him. "And I see what you're doing. You're answering a question with a question."

He forced a grin. "Must be the journalist in me."

"Have you ever been a reporter?"

"While I was working on my doctorate—years ago. You would have been just a baby at the time," he said, needing to add the last sentence to remind him of their age difference.

"Yes, that's right. You're ancient." Cassie tapped her chin. "Let's see. You're what? Ten? Twelve years older than I am? Definitely ancient."

He chuckled. "Okay, you've made your point. I'm not *that* much older than you in years." He left unsaid how much older he felt in experience. There was an innocence about Cassie that she'd retained even after ten years in the real world. He yearned for that and realized he'd never been that way, even as a child.

"Well, I'm glad we've got that settled. The next thing I know they'll refuse to let me vote."

"Most women would love to be thought of as younger than they are."

"I'm not most women."

That's so true. He was tempted to discover what she'd been doing for the past ten years. When Scott had been in his class, he'd told him about Cassie working at a high school as a physical education teacher and coaching gymnastics. But that was when she had lived in Savannah. What was she doing back here in Magnolia Falls? The same thing? He started to ask and immediately stamped down his curiosity.

"We'd better go back inside before they send out a search party," he said, instead of asking all the questions he wanted to know the answers to, questions he had no business asking.

"Dinner should be served shortly. As usual Steff has outdone herself with the preparations."

Jameson walked beside Cassie toward the door into the inn. "Steff Kessler was the perfect choice to be alumni director."

At the entrance into the Event Hall Cassie turned toward him when he stopped. "Steff certainly has the connections. I think a third of the buildings at the college are named after someone in her family." She started into the room, noticed he hadn't followed and swung back around. "Aren't you coming in?"

"I'm not staying for dinner." He allowed his gaze to take in her black silk dress that fell in soft folds around her knees. She looked elegant and beautiful.

"Why not?" Disappointment furrowed her brow.

The urge to smooth the creases from her forehead inundated him, confirming his need to leave. "I've played hooky from writing long enough. Good night." He pivoted and strode away before he could change his mind. Cassie was a delightful, intelligent woman. He didn't need that complication in his life.

TWO

Two months later

"I come all the way to Magnolia Falls and you're heading out the door." Scott blocked Cassie's way.

Stepping back, she looked up into her little brother's face and dropped her purse on the table next to the front door. "If you had bothered to call before coming, I would have told you I'm taking a night class at the college."

"Oh? Are you going for another master's?" He moved into the foyer, backing her up a few paces.

"No, I'm just taking one of the short courses they offer at the college." She checked her watch. "Which will start in half an hour. I'd rather not be late."

"What class?"

"Nothing too exciting." Cassie waved her hand in dismissal, hoping her brother didn't pursue the question.

His laughter ruffled her feathers. "I'm a reporter. You can't be evasive with me."

She reached around him and snatched up her purse. "Yes, I can. If you want to make yourself at home, go ahead. I'll be back in a few hours."

"Nah. I have to meet someone in a while. I just wanted

to say hi. Now that you live in Magnolia Falls, I don't get to see you as much."

"Savannah's only an hour away. You're welcome anytime. This is your home, too."

"By the way, where's Mom?" He peered over her shoulder toward the living room.

"At the neighbors'. She's finally going out for an evening since she got sick." Cassie skirted around her younger brother and headed out onto the porch. A nagging sensation made her pause and turn back toward Scott. "Did you want to talk to me about something?"

A brief glimpse of sadness and tiny lines creasing his forehead aged him beyond his twenty-five years. "No, it can wait. We'll talk another time when you're not hurrying out the door."

"Are you sure?" She felt suddenly reluctant to leave.

"Yes." He shooed her away. "Go to your mysterious class."

While she descended the steps, she heard Scott say behind her, "I intend to find out what you're taking. There should be no secrets between us."

She turned and backpedaled toward her car in the driveway. "Who are you meeting?"

"No one of importance to you."

She grinned. "It looks like we both have our secrets."

His chuckles followed her to her white Taurus. She refused to look toward him as she slid behind the steering wheel and left. Her brother already knew how interested she was in Dr. Jameson King. She could imagine the ribbing she would receive if Scott knew she was taking a night class taught by his mentor. She would never hear the end of it. But after seeing Jameson at the fund-raiser a few months ago, she had decided it was a sign. Life was too short. He was no longer married, and she was no longer his student—well, his college student. Now that it was October and she was settled into her new job at the local high school, she had some time in the evening.

Fifteen minutes later she parked in a space near the campus building where the class was being taught and hurried toward the Gothic structure. She didn't want to be late for Jameson's class on persuasive writing. Seeing him again reminded her how much she'd enjoyed his lectures, especially listening to his deep voice as he expounded on a subject he was passionate about.

Cassie slipped inside the lecture hall on the second floor as Jameson approached the front. Dressed in tan slacks and a black, long-sleeved shirt, he paused by the table and dropped his notepad, then scanned the audience. His gaze fell on her, and a smile gleamed in his eyes. She quickly settled in a desk in the last row and listened as the rich sound of his voice filled the room.

For the next two hours Jameson mesmerized her. Before she knew it, the students around her were standing and gathering their books and papers to leave.

Taking a composing breath, she rose and made her way toward the front. She waited while a few classmates spoke to Jameson. When the last one left, she stepped in front of him, and suddenly everyone else faded from her consciousness except Jameson King.

He removed the wire-rimmed glasses he used for reading and stuck them in a pocket. "What a pleasant surprise to see you taking one of my classes again. Have you decided to come back to college?"

She shook her head. "I just took advantage of the auditing program the college has for the townspeople. I figured I could use some persuasive techniques to get my mentoring program started at the high school."

"I thought for a moment you might be following in your brother's footsteps and going into journalism."

"I'll leave the reporting to him. He likes to dig for answers, not me."

"And he's very good at what he does. I liked his last series of articles about the effects of the high cost of health insurance on the ordinary person." Jameson collected his notes.

"I thought I was the only one who followed Scott's career."

He started for the door. "I read six or seven newspapers a day. The Savannah paper is one of them. I particularly like to read any work by a former student of mine." He allowed her to go first into the hallway.

"Does everyone still go to the Half Joe for coffee after classes?"

"Yes. Some traditions haven't changed."

"Would you care to join me there, then? I haven't been since I returned to Magnolia Falls, and I spent many days and nights there studying and cramming for exams."

"Sure. I only planned to go home and grade some essays."

Outside the English building the warm October night with a hint of honeysuckle in the air enveloped Cassie. A full moon hung in the sky, its brightness obscuring the stars nearby.

Jameson peered toward the parking lot at the side of the building, then toward the road. "Since it's not far, do you want to walk?"

"That sounds nice."

"How's your new job going? Do you like it as much

as your old one in Savannah?" Jameson asked as they crossed the street.

"I love it. I'm a counselor at the high school. I really enjoy counseling teenagers. And the girls I work with on the gymnastics team are talented and eager to learn."

He made an tsking sound. "You're beginning to sound like me."

"I'll take that as a compliment."

He looked at her directly as he opened the café's door for her. "I've found if you have passion for what you teach, it's hard not to convey that to your students. Before you know it, they're feeling the same way."

Entering the Half Joe, Cassie scanned the college hangout for an empty chair or couch. She spied her brother sitting off in the corner with two tall men, probably a few years younger than Scott.

"Ah, I see your brother is here. Now, that brings back some memories. We used to come here after class and have some lively conversations."

A group near her brother rose from a worn brown leather couch. Cassie pointed toward it. "Let's grab it before someone else does."

As she wound her way through the maze of chairs and couches, she heard several people call out to Jameson. Her brother glanced up and saw them. Frowning, he returned his attention to the two young men he was talking to. He jotted something on a notepad on the table in front of him.

Strange, Cassie thought, taking in the tension in Scott's posture, the intensity in his expression. A minute ago she had been tempted to interrupt their conversation, but something warned her that her little brother wouldn't be too happy with her, as though he was on assignment and nothing should interfere with his interview.

When she sat on the couch, Jameson settled next to her and waved his hand for the waitress. "What would you like?"

"A cup of green tea."

When the college-age woman stopped on the other side of the table in front of the couch, Jameson gave her their orders.

The waitress's expression brightened. "Anything else, Dr. King? We have freshly baked white-chocolate-and-macadamia nut cookies. I know how much you like those."

He patted his flat stomach. "I'm afraid too much. Not tonight."

"It's obvious you still frequent this place," Cassie said when the young woman left.

"I wrote part of my book here."

"You did? The noise wasn't distracting?"

"I'm very good at tuning others out when I need to. But I found inspiration watching the different people, especially when I got stuck."

"When is your book coming out?" Cassie pushed her hair behind her ears.

"Not for another year."

"Why a murder mystery?"

"When I worked as a reporter, I covered several murder cases from beginning to end, so I drew on my experience."

"Write about what you know?"

His smile transformed his face, erasing the hint of sadness she often saw lurking in the depths of his eyes.

"I can't say I've actually been involved in a murder case. Just as an observer."

"And now we have our very own murder case at the college." A tremor snaked down Cassie's spine when she thought about the unknown woman found in August who was still unidentified.

The waitress placed their orders on the coffee table in front of them, giving Jameson a big grin and a shy once-over before leaving. Cassie wondered if the young woman had taken any of Jameson's classes. He seemed oblivious to his effect on the female population, but she'd seen the look on the waitress's face and knew what it meant. When she had been in his class years ago she'd probably had the same silly grin on her face.

He took his mug and sipped his drink. "Even though it's been nearly two months, everyone is still talking about the murdered woman."

"People love a good mystery."

"That's what I'm hoping with my novel."

"Thinking of giving up teaching when you become a success?"

"First, most writers don't make a decent living with their writing, and second, the business is fickle." He drank a swallow of his coffee. "Now, it's my turn. Why are you taking my class?"

She'd always been straightforward, and this time she couldn't be any less than that. "When I saw you at the fund-raiser, I remembered how much I enjoyed your classes, so I signed up when this short course became available. As a teacher I can always use persuasive techniques in dealing with students."

She curled her hands around her mug of tea, her gaze drifting toward her brother, engrossed in a conversation with the two young men. The impression he was working on a story was still strong. So what did these two students have to do with it?

"When we came in, you seemed surprised to see Scott here."

Jameson's observation drew her attention back to the man beside her on the couch. "Yes. He stopped by the house earlier, but he didn't say anything about coming here."

"In the past month I've seen him here several times."

"You have?"

"Yeah. You didn't know he was visiting Magnolia Falls?"

"No." Again she glanced toward Scott. What was he up to? "Is he meeting with the same people?"

"No, different ones. But I've found most of them are connected with the basketball team. I thought at first he might be helping out this season. Practice has started, and although he couldn't go pro, he can still play."

"But he doesn't. When the accident happened, he blamed himself for the team not going any further in the NCAA tournament that year."

"If I remember correctly, we had a good chance of winning the tournament."

Cassie felt uncomfortable being reminded of that awful time four years ago when her brother's life came crashing down around him.

"Granted, Scott was the star player, but as I told him then, he was only one member of the team. Winning is a team effort and so is losing."

"I said basically the same thing to him, but it didn't make any difference. He walked away from the game. He rarely even watches it. So why is he talking to members of the team?"

Jameson arched an eyebrow, a gleam glinting in his eyes. "A good question. A story?"

"Possibly. Is there a player who has a chance to go to the NBA?"

"I gather you don't follow basketball, either."

"No, just gymnastics. I only followed it when Scott played."

Jameson tilted his head to the side and thought for a moment. "Maybe. There's one who has a shot. Marcus Reed. He's a junior."

"Reed? Any relation to the Kevin Reed who was involved in Scott's injury on the basketball court?"

"His younger brother. He has a lot more talent than Kevin did."

"Is Marcus one of the young men he's with?"

"No, but a reporter often interviews people around a subject."

"Then maybe he's doing a story on Marcus. If so, that's a good thing." Cassie finished the last sip of her tea.

"Why?"

"I didn't think it was good that Scott walked away from basketball altogether. He lived and breathed it before the accident. He also harbored a lot of anger toward Kevin because of what happened. They were best friends, and now Kevin has dropped off the face of the earth."

"I imagine Kevin had a hard time dealing with the accident, too. Sometimes when something is too painful, you have to cut yourself off totally in order to survive."

Cassie suddenly realized they weren't just talking about her brother and Kevin. What had been so painful in Jameson's life? His wife's death had occurred almost a year ago, and yet she'd sensed that deep pain even back when she had been in his class as a college student. "You can't run forever. You have to face the problem and deal with it. It won't go away."

A distant look dimmed his eyes. "True."

So intent on Jameson, she didn't hear or see her brother approach until he cleared his throat and said, "Cassie, I didn't know you were going to be here. I thought you were taking a class…."

Her gaze swept to Scott on the other side of the coffee table. "I am. I signed up for Jameson's persuasive writing class."

Her brother's glance fell on his mentor, then back to Cassie. "You forgot to mention that."

"And you forgot to mention you've been coming to Magnolia Falls on a regular basis. Working on a story?"

Scott's expression went blank. "I'm always working on a story. Well, I'd better be going. I still have to drive back to Savannah. It's good to see you, Jameson." He nodded toward them, then left before Cassie could say anything else.

"I think I scared him off with my question."

"I think you did, too." Jameson stared at Scott as he made his way toward the door. "As much as I've enjoyed this, I have papers to grade. May I walk you to your car?"

When he removed his wallet to pay, Cassie put her hand over his, stopping him. The touch singed her fingertips. "This is my treat. I invited you."

He started to say something but looked into her eyes and decided not to. Sliding his wallet back into his pocket, he rose. "Thanks. Next time will be my treat."

The idea there could be another time made her heart

flutter. Then she caught sight of his wedding ring that he still wore. The glittering gold taunted her.

His gaze trapped her full attention, and all thoughts fled her mind. She wanted to get to know him beyond the nice pleasantries they had shared. In college she'd had a simple schoolgirl's crush on her handsome professor. Now she realized it could be so much more, but it was obvious he was still very much in love with his deceased wife.

"I'll hold you to that," she murmured finally.

A few minutes later Cassie stepped outside with Jameson at her side. Aware of his every move, she crossed the street and strolled back toward the parking lot on campus where their cars were.

At her Taurus she unlocked its door, then faced him. He was only a foot away, and she could smell his fresh, clean scent in the night air. She saw him cock a grin, making him appear younger, carefree.

"Thanks for the coffee."

"You're welcome." She didn't want the evening to end, but his demeanor had suddenly become one of a polite stranger, as though he suddenly realized how alone they were.

"Good night. See you next week in class."

She slipped inside her car and watched him disappear into the darkness at the other end of the parking lot. Gripping the steering wheel, she laid her head on the cold plastic and dragged air into her lungs. Why did she feel as though she were playing with fire?

Lord, he's hurting. Please take his pain away.

As she passed the Half Joe, Cassie glanced toward its parking lot on the right side of the building. The security light shone down on her brother standing in front of a tall young man she didn't know. Scott waved his arm and pointed toward the campus. Cassie slowed her car. A scowl on his face, the young man shook his head and stalked toward the entrance into the café. Clearly frustrated, Scott pounded his fist on the top of his vehicle.

Cassie started to make a U-turn to go back to see what was wrong with her brother, when he wrenched open his door, got into his car and pulled out of the parking lot, heading in the opposite direction.

What just happened?

Stopping at a red light, Cassie looked in her rearview mirror as though the deserted street would give her answers. They were both keeping secrets. Maybe she and her brother were more alike than she had ever thought.

At his apartment Jameson sat at the desk in his office, staring at the same paper he had been reading for the past half hour. He'd marked a few comments at the beginning, but after rereading the same paragraph several times, he realized he might as well call it quits. He wasn't going to be able to grade papers tonight. His mind kept wandering back to this evening at the Half Joe with Cassie. Why had he accepted her invitation? He shouldn't have.

He knew the danger in getting too close to someone like her. She was as beautiful and vivacious as he remembered her ten years before. Actually, even more so. Now she was a woman who had experienced life and hadn't been marred by its harsh realities.

He lounged back in his chair, a vision of Cassie forming in his mind. Red shoulder-length hair and bright emerald-green eyes a man could get lost in. He scrubbed his hands down his face and shot to his feet. Restless energy surged through him. He needed to get away for a couple of days.

How could he think of Cassie in that way? He had no right to, although his wife had died nearly a year ago after being in a coma for twelve years. But if it hadn't been for him, Liz would still be alive. He'd carry that guilt to the grave.

He strode into his bedroom across the hall and snatched up a duffel bag. After stuffing a few extra pieces of clothing into it, he zipped it up and grabbed his car keys. He'd drive up the coast, clear his head.

As he walked toward the front door, his phone rang. He paused and started toward the table to pick it up. Halfway there, he stopped and let it continue to ring. Finally his answering machine picked up the call.

"Jameson, this is Scott. After seeing you tonight at the café, I knew I needed to talk to you about this story I'm working on. Please call me as soon as you can."

Jameson reached for the receiver and froze, his wedding ring he still wore ridiculing him. No. He couldn't deal with Cassie's brother right now. Scott looked so much like Cassie. He would speak to the young man when he came back tomorrow evening—after he'd closed his heart to her.

THREE

Friday night Jameson tossed his duffel bag onto his bed and glanced at his answering machine. Three messages. Sinking down onto the covers, he pushed the button to listen to the recording.

"This is Scott. I was checking to see if you were home since you weren't at the college. I want to come by to talk to you." The time of that call was noon.

Jameson pressed the next message left three hours ago.

"I'm on to something big. I need your advice. I may be too close to this. Call as soon as you can. I *have* to talk to you. If I'm not here, my calls are being forwarded to my cell so I'll be available."

Jameson lifted his receiver and punched in Cassie's brother's number. When he didn't pick up, Jameson told him to call as soon as he could, that he would be at home. Then realizing he had another message, Jameson listened to the last one, left only a half an hour before.

"Jameson! Where are you?" Jameson heard a sound in the background, but he couldn't tell what it was. "Call! I need to talk—" The line went dead.

Had someone interrupted Scott? The message ended so abruptly.

Concern seeped into Jameson. He replayed the message, but still couldn't figure out what the noise was. He tried both Scott's cell and his apartment, but again no answer. Why didn't Scott pick up on his cell if he was waiting for him to call? Maybe Scott hung up earlier because he was angry that he wasn't home. That could explain the sudden end to the message.

But what was that noise? Maybe Scott was pacing and knocked into something.

Unease nagged Jameson as he trudged toward the kitchen to make a pot of coffee. He needed to grade those papers. He would do that while he waited for Scott to return his call. Maybe he was busy and couldn't answer. Scott was a reporter and a grown man. He could certainly take care of himself, but there was something in his voice that…

He shook off his worry, remembering when he'd been a reporter and working a case. Sometimes he would lose track of time and become so focused on the story that nothing else mattered, not even eating.

After fixing a mug, Jameson took it into his office and settled down to work. But as he stared at the stack of essays, his mind was filled with his unsuccessful trip up the coast. Cassie's smile still dominated his thoughts. She was a breath of fresh air in his stale life. For the past twelve years he had been going through the motions of living, but how could he have gone on with his life when Liz was in a coma because of him?

The phone blared, jerking Jameson out of his reverie. He grabbed it on the second ring, expecting it to be Scott. So when he heard Cassie, surprise—and something he didn't want to acknowledge—flowed through him.

"Jameson, I'm sorry to bother you, but I wasn't sure

what to do. Scott called over three hours ago and said he was coming to Magnolia Falls. He said he needed to talk to us and then see you. We haven't seen him. Is he there?"

"No, I haven't talked to him, but he did leave me several messages."

"I know I shouldn't be worried, but…" There was a long pause, then in a low voice Cassie said, "Scott didn't sound right. Something's wrong."

He didn't want to mention it, but he had to. "Have you checked with the highway patrol?"

"I hadn't thought about that. I'll call them," she whispered, her distress conveyed in her hushed tone.

Remembering the urgency in Scott's voice in the last message prompted Jameson to say, "I'll come over. That way if he shows up I'll be there, and we can talk then."

"Thanks."

Her gratefulness pushed to the background all his doubts about the wisdom of seeing her again. In his gut he knew something was wrong. He'd gotten this feeling several times when he had been a reporter and each time it had been dead-on. The last message from Scott had sounded almost frantic—not like the young man he knew. What kind of story was he working on? Why did Scott need to talk to him?

Cassie looked toward her mother sitting at the kitchen table, worry lining her face. "Jameson is coming over." She picked up the phone again and called the highway patrol. As she asked if there were any accidents on the road between Savannah and Magnolia Falls, her mother's expression darkened.

"Were there any?" Victoria Winters asked when Cassie replaced the receiver in its cradle.

"No."

"Try Scott again."

"I've already called and left four messages."

Her mother rose and leaned into the table with her fists on its wooden top. "Try."

Cassie called but didn't bother to leave another message. Something was wrong. They both knew it but neither wanted to say it out loud. Not showing up when he'd said he would was something he had done back when he had been drinking heavily.

She could remember one time in particular a couple of years ago when her mother had insisted she go over to Scott's apartment after he hadn't shown up for a job interview with a friend of the family. She had found him passed out on the floor, completely unresponsive. The doctor had later said that if she hadn't gotten him medical help when she had, he would have died.

"Something else probably came up. The life of a reporter can be unpredictable," Cassie offered.

Her mom shook her head. "No. No, that isn't it. He made it a point to make sure we would be here so he could talk to us. Something else has happened, Cassie. I know it in here." She tapped her chest over her heart. "I don't get this feeling often, but when I do, there is always something wrong."

Cassie wanted to argue the point with her but couldn't find the words. Her mother was right. The few times she had insisted something was wrong, it had been. "What do you want to do? Call the police?"

Her mother's eyes grew round, and she sank down onto the chair. "The police? If for some reason Scott has started drinking again, he would be so upset that we—"

The doorbell chimed. "That's probably Jameson. I'll be right back."

On her way out of the kitchen she heard her mother mutter, "He's such a nice young man. Maybe he can help us find Scott."

Cassie opened the front door and found Jameson King filling her entrance with his large presence. Relief flooded her as she stared into his blue eyes. "Come in. Scott still hasn't called or shown up, and Mom is beside herself. She's in the kitchen."

Jameson followed her into the room and greeted her mother with a smile. "I'm sure Scott's all right, Mrs. Winters."

"No, he isn't." Her mother swung her tear-misted gaze to Cassie. "You should go to Savannah and check on him. Please. This sitting around waiting is driving me crazy."

"Sure, Mom, and if he comes here, call me on my cell." Her heart wrenched seeing her mother so upset. "Why don't you lie down and rest? I'll call you when I get to Scott's apartment."

"I won't sleep until you let me know he's fine. In fact—" she started for the counter where her purse sat "—I'm going with you. I don't want you going alone."

"Mom, you've been sick. I've driven back and forth from here to Savannah so many times I could do it blindfolded."

"Darling, I don't think you—"

"Mrs. Winters, I'll drive Cassie to Scott's. You don't have to worry about a thing."

Her mother fastened her attention on Jameson. "You will?"

"Yes, ma'am."

"You see, I'll be fine." Cassie took her mother's arm

and led her toward the living room. "So while I'm gone, promise me you'll put your feet up in your lounger and rest, or I won't go."

Her mom's mouth pinched into a frown. "I don't like being blackmailed."

"I wouldn't have to resort to it if you'd follow your doctor's orders. You did too much today." Cassie helped settle her into the comfortable chair, then put the footrest up for her. "I'm a phone call away if you need me or if Scott finally shows up." She pulled her cell out of her jeans pocket to emphasize the point.

Her mother waved her hand. "Go, y'all. Now."

Five minutes later Cassie sat next to Jameson in his car as he backed out of the driveway and headed toward the highway. For a moment she let the silence lengthen while she calmed herself. Her mother's recent bout with pneumonia worried Cassie more than Scott's lateness.

"Thanks for going to Savannah with me," she said, needing to take her mind off her mother's failing health. She was in God's hands. He would care for her. "When Mom insists on something, nothing can change her mind. I'm sure that's where my brother got his stubbornness."

"But not you?"

"I'm not stubborn. I'm pretty laid-back."

"How did that happen with a brother and mother who aren't?"

"That's why I am. Someone has to give in or you live in angst all the time. Not good for you."

On the highway the gray of dusk cloaked the landscape in shadows. The sun sank below the tree line, coloring the pale blue sky with orange, yellow and rose. Soon it would be dark, and Cassie was secretly glad that Jameson had volunteered to drive her to Savannah. Her vivid imagination could get the best of her.

"I can't imagine what Scott wanted to talk to Mom and me about. He didn't give you any indication?"

"I got the impression it concerned a story he's working on."

"But then why would he want to talk to us? Do you think it had something to do with those students on the basketball team that he interviewed the other day? Or maybe the skeleton found under the library sidewalk? That would be a story Scott would go after."

He shrugged. "It could be. That's the first question we can ask him when we find him."

Each time Jameson said "we" her smile grew. She liked the sound of it. "I just hope we don't pass him on the highway."

"What kind of car does he drive? I'll keep an eye out for it."

"A 1966 red Ford Mustang."

"That shouldn't be too hard to spot. At least not until it gets dark."

"We'll be on the outskirts of Savannah by that time." Which was probably about thirty minutes away.

As silence engulfed the car again, Cassie searched her mind for a new topic of conversation. There was so much she wanted to know about Jameson, now that she had him as a captive audience. "So, where are you from originally? Where were you a reporter?"

"New York City."

"One of the big papers?"

He nodded. "*The Times.*"

She whistled. "What made you give it up?"

"It was time to move on." His tone indicated he wasn't going to offer more information than that.

"Why did you come to Magnolia College?"

"It has a good journalism department."

"A lot of colleges do. How'd you hear about the school?"

Cassie couldn't help noticing his stiff posture and tight grip on the steering wheel. "I thought I was the reporter. Are you sure you don't want to be one?"

Realizing she sounded as though she were interrogating him, she laughed, hoping to ease his strain. "I guess my brother has rubbed off on me more than I thought." Although she attempted to lighten the mood, she was aware of the growing awkwardness in the car. Jameson was hiding something. Did it have to do with his deceased wife? She peered at his gold wedding band, barely visible in the dim dashboard lights.

"Now it's my turn. What made you come back to Magnolia Falls after living in Savannah for years?"

"As you saw tonight, Mom isn't well. Both Scott and I felt she needed someone to look after her. I was the one who could move the easiest."

"Did you mind coming back?"

She thought for a moment about the question. At first she had resisted Scott's suggestion, but it hadn't taken her long to realize she'd loved growing up in the small college town, and coming home would be good for her as well as her mother. "No, it was time for me to come home."

"How does your mother feel about it?"

"She was relieved, which made me realize she was sicker than both Scott and I originally thought. Are your parents alive?"

"Both alive and well in Florida. Retired and having a ball."

The lights of Savannah lit the dark horizon. Soon they would be at Scott's apartment, and there was a part of Cassie that wanted this drive to last longer. She'd found out more about Jameson than she ever had before, but really it was only facts. She wanted to know so much more. But first she needed to check on her brother and put her mother's mind at ease.

"Where does your brother live?"

She gave him Scott's address, then the direction to his apartment. Silence fell between them again when they hit Savannah. The closer she got to her brother's, the more the tension built inside her. She remembered the times she'd find him drunk and barely able to stand. With the Lord's help she'd managed to get Scott to attend his first AA meeting. Thankfully he'd now been sober for more than a year and focused on his job at the paper. Scott was a pit bull when working on a story, and she was sure he'd just gotten sidetracked—that this one time her mother's hunch was wrong.

Jameson parked out in front of the large white house that had been converted into apartments in an older section of the city. The serenity of the neighborhood appeased Cassie's anxiety. Soon she would discover they had overreacted and have to explain their sudden appearance to her brother.

Standing on the sidewalk in front, Cassie pointed down the driveway. "Scott's place is over the garage." She started for the back. "He likes his privacy." Which reminded her instantly of the man walking beside her.

She mounted the stairs on the back of the building and

knocked on her brother's door. Nothing, although the lights blazed from his windows.

"Do you have a key?"

"No. I used to with the old apartment." There hadn't been a need since Scott had stopped drinking.

Jameson glanced around, saw a window a few feet from the landing and stretched over the railing to peer inside. "Try the door."

Panic bolted through her at the urgency in his words. She tried turning the knob. "It's locked. What's wrong?"

"He's on the floor. A bottle of whiskey is on the coffee table nearby. Almost empty."

"No!" *Scott's drinking again? If so, how can he be so drunk that he passed out this quickly?*

Jameson straightened. "Does the manager have a key?"

"Yes." She tried to look in the window and wasn't tall enough to reach it. "Mrs. Alexander has an apartment on the first floor."

"Let's go get her."

Cassie hurried down the stairs and ran toward the house. Inside the large foyer, she quickly crossed it and pounded on the manager's door. A minute ticked by. Her heart beat a maddening pace. She lifted her hand to knock again when the door opened, and Mrs. Alexander greeted her with a smile that faded quickly when she stared at Cassie.

"Sugar, what's wrong?"

"Scott's hurt in his apartment, and I can't get in."

"Let me get my keys." The older woman disappeared inside her place for a long moment before returning. "Sorry. I had a hard time finding his. It wasn't where I usually keep it, which is strange. I must get more absent-minded as I get older."

Jameson's presence behind Cassie soothed her as they rushed back to Scott's as fast as Mrs. Alexander could go. Beads of sweat popped out on Cassie's forehead as the older woman inserted the key into the lock.

Please, Lord, let Scott be all right.

As Mrs. Alexander shoved the door open, Cassie and Jameson hurried past her. The scent of whiskey—and something else she couldn't identify—hung in the air. Sprawled on the floor by the coffee table lay Scott on his left side, not moving. As she knelt by her brother, Cassie noticed the amber liquid in the bottle. So little left.

With a trembling hand, she reached out to turn Scott over, faceup. Blood covered the left side of his head from a deep gash. For a few seconds her gaze stayed riveted to the red stain on the carpet before she could drag her attention away. When she caught sight of his open eyes staring lifelessly at her, she put her quivering fingers on the side of his neck to find his pulse.

"Please be alive. Please," she whispered.

His skin had a bluish tinge and felt cold. She couldn't find a pulse. "Call 911." She looked up at Jameson. "Do you know CPR?"

He squatted on the other side of Scott. His expression, full of concern, filled her vision. He took her hand and held it.

"Cassie, it's too late."

"No, we can save him," she said while Mrs. Alexander shuffled toward the phone to call 911.

"He's dead." Jameson stood, bringing her up with him.

She went into his arms, desperately needing the

comfort. "I don't understand. I talked to him less than four hours ago and he was fine. How can he be dead?"

Jameson didn't say anything for a long moment. Finally he leaned down and whispered into her ear, "I don't know, Cassie, but we'll find out why this happened."

"Why?" She pulled back. "He started drinking again and must have tripped and hit his head. He..." Words clogged her throat.

"Cassie, we don't know anything for sure." He smoothed her hair back behind her ears and cupped her face.

Remembering all the times she had sat with her brother and nursed him after a drinking binge, she shook her head and stepped away from the solace of Jameson's touch. "I've been through this before. Except..." She cleared her throat. "This time I didn't come in time. I should have been here hours ago."

"Sugar—" Mrs. Alexander placed her hand on her arm "—the police are on their way."

The police! Of course they had to come, but their arrival made this whole horrible situation true, not some bad nightmare she could wake up from. "What made him start drinking again?" Cassie swept her gaze from the manager to Jameson, fighting the urge to go back into his embrace. "Why didn't he come to Magnolia Falls like he said he was? What made him change his mind?"

"I don't have any answers, Cassie."

"Sugar, I'll wait for the police out front." With a frown, Mrs. Alexander backed away, avoiding looking at Scott on the floor.

As Cassie watched the manager hurry from the apartment, the trembling started in her hands and rapidly spread through her whole body. She wrapped her arms around herself, but a blanket of cold encased her. "He had so much to live for. He never could hold his liquor well." She sucked in one deep breath after another, but nothing filled her oxygen-deprived lungs.

Jameson encircled her in his embrace and drew her back against him. His breath fanned her neck. "Cassie, let's go outside on the landing and wait for the police."

She twisted around. "No. I can't leave him alone. I should have been here earlier."

"You didn't know this was going to happen. You can't blame yourself."

The fervent tone of his voice took her by surprise. She stared into his blue eyes and saw a storm of emotions that rivaled hers. Glancing beyond him, she spied Scott on the floor, his color leached from his face. Seeing him confirmed what she'd known when she had touched him the first time: her brother was dead.

"How am I going to tell Mom?"

"I'll come with you, if you want."

She swung her attention back to Jameson. "You will?"

He nodded.

Mrs. Alexander entered the apartment with two police officers. She gestured toward Scott. "We found him like that."

The older of the two surveyed the room, then fixed his sharp gaze upon Cassie and Jameson. "Are y'all the ones who asked Mrs. Alexander to unlock the door?"

Her mouth dry, Cassie started to answer the officer, but no words came out.

Instead, Jameson said, "Yes. We came to check on Miss Winters's brother."

A look passed between the two officers, then the older one indicated the entrance. "Let's talk outside." He waited for all three of them to exit the apartment first.

As Cassie stood on the small landing, the warm air did nothing to thaw the icy feeling that coursed through her. She gritted her teeth to keep them from chattering and nearly jumped when Jameson placed his hand at the small of her back.

"Are you okay?"

Cassie gave Jameson a quick nod, although she wasn't sure of anything. Her mind reeled.

"Mrs. Alexander, may we use your apartment to interview y'all?" the older policeman asked in a thick, Southern drawl.

"Yes." The manager descended the stairs first.

Aware of his hand still touching her as though imparting some of his strength to her, Cassie followed with Jameson right behind her.

"I have to call Mom." Sorrow squeezed her throat tightly, causing her voice to thicken. She knew from past experience she wouldn't shed any tears—she'd learned long ago not to—but that didn't stop her from feeling a deep sadness.

Jameson glanced back at the officer behind him. "Miss Winters needs to let her mother know what has happened."

"After I talk with y'all, she can call her."

Cassie halted and faced the older man. "She's expecting my call. She's the one who sent us here to check on Scott."

"Why?"

"Because she was worried. He was supposed to be at

our house a few hours ago, but he didn't show up or answer his cell." Under the police officer's survey, she felt like a suspect being assessed.

Before the man could say anything, Cassie's phone rang. She withdrew it from her pocket and looked toward the police officer. "It's her calling."

"Answer it. We'll be inside." The man mounted the steps to the porch with Mrs. Alexander.

Cassie's hand quivered as she punched the On button. Her heart pounded. Dread covered her in a sheen of sweat. "Mom," she said into the cell, her gaze glued to Jameson.

"Where's Scott, Cassie?"

Jameson's calming presence slowed the beating of her heart enough that she could answer, "He's not with me." She realized this wasn't the way to tell her mother.

"He's not there? Where is he?"

With the Lord, Cassie thought, but couldn't say that out loud. She didn't want her mother to be alone when she found out about Scott, especially in her precarious health.

"Mom, Jameson and I will be home shortly. We'll figure out what's going on." She disconnected the cell before her mother pursued the conversation. She couldn't out and out lie to her mom.

Jameson clasped her hand, his eyes full of sadness.

"I couldn't tell her over the phone. We need to get back to Magnolia Falls as soon as possible. I have to be there when she's told."

"Then let's wrap this up and head back." His arm went around her shoulder.

She leaned into him as they entered the building. The

officer was waiting for them in the doorway to Mrs. Alexander's apartment, looking at them both grimly.

"Miss Winters, my partner just called from your brother's place. Something doesn't add up with your brother's death."

FOUR

Jameson stepped forward. "You think there may have been foul play?"

"It's a possibility. Until we know more, we're handling it as a murder investigation."

"Scott murdered?" The words staggered Cassie. Jameson clasped her against him as her legs gave way. "How—I mean..." She didn't know what to say. Thoughts that made no sense tumbled through her mind.

"Why does your partner think that?" Jameson tightened his hold on her.

"We'll know more after our forensics team goes over the crime scene and we get the autopsy report."

"Crime scene," Cassie whispered, her throat raw with emotion.

"Let's go inside and talk." The police officer stepped to the side to allow Cassie and Jameson to enter the apartment.

He started forward.

Cassie hung back, frozen to the spot. "I can't do this. I need to get home and tell Mom. I don't want her to hear from anyone but me."

"Ma'am, I understand. I'll try to get you home as

quickly as possible." The young man went first through the entrance into Mrs. Alexander's place.

"Cassie?"

The concern in Jameson's voice touched the icy grip on her heart. She took a deep, fortifying breath and moved into the apartment.

The aroma of coffee drifted to her. Such an ordinary smell. Then Cassie remembered the other scents that accosted her in Scott's living room—whiskey, blood. She shuddered.

Mrs. Alexander bustled out of the kitchen. "I've put a pot of coffee on. Would anyone like a cup?"

Cassie's stomach churned, and she shook her head.

"I'll take one." Jameson guided her toward the couch and sat.

"Sure," the officer said to Mrs. Alexander, who immediately went back into the kitchen. He sank into a chair across from Cassie and Jameson and opened his pad. "Tell me what happened."

Exhausted beyond sleep, Cassie trudged into the kitchen, so glad to see Jameson still at the house even though it was well past midnight. He glanced up, quickly masking the apprehension in his expression.

"How's your mom?" He cradled his mug and brought it to his lips to take a sip.

Cassie eased down into the chair next to him. "Finally asleep."

He held up his cup. "Do you want any coffee?"

"No, can't stand the stuff." She stared at the oak tabletop, trying to put some kind of order to her thoughts. The sound of her mother's sobs still crowded her mind. Someone did this to her family. She curled her hands into fists, her fingernails digging into her palms. "I want to find whoever did this and make him pay."

"The police will be looking into Scott's death. It hasn't been ruled a murder yet."

"So you think he simply fell and hit his head on the table?"

"There was blood on the edge of it and on nothing else—at least that I could see." The last few words were spoken with less conviction that it wasn't murder.

"Maybe the killer took it with him."

"You would rather Scott had been murdered than drinking again?"

"No, of course..." She tightened her hands even more until her knuckles stood out, white. "I don't know what to think anymore. But that officer was suspicious."

"I don't think it's just because Scott had liquor all over the front of his shirt. He could have spilled that on himself. Whatever it is, the police aren't saying. Maybe it's just a gut feeling."

She remembered one time that her brother had been so drunk he had done that very thing. Which was worse? Her brother drinking himself to death or someone killing him?

Jameson covered her hands with his. "Let's give the police a chance. They'll know more after the autopsy. His blood alcohol level will indicate whether he was drinking or not."

Anger that held her stiff siphoned from her, and she sagged against the table. "I had to listen to my mother cry herself to sleep. We had come through so much with Scott. He was getting his life back on track finally. What if someone came along and ended it—" she snapped her fingers "—just like that. It could be tied to a story he was working on."

"Why do you say that?" Jameson downed the last swig of his drink.

"All the questions about whether Scott worked at home or not, how he kept notes on a story he was investigating. Right before we left, I overheard one of the detectives say he was going down to the newspaper next."

"That could mean anything. Scott had already gained quite a reputation for digging until he discovered the whole truth. He'd made a few people unhappy with some of his stories."

Cassie scraped the chair back and shot to her feet. "Exactly! Scott could have made someone angry with one of his pieces, and he got even by killing him."

"That's a possibility, and the police will look into it. But they're also asking questions about Scott and his drinking."

Leaning forward, she rested her knuckles on the plaid place mat. "After the scene is processed, they want me to go through Scott's place and see if anything is missing."

"The police need to rule out robbery as a motive, if he was murdered."

The thought of going through her brother's possessions, knowing she would have to box them up soon, chilled her. "I—I know, but..."

Jameson rose. "Do you want me to go with you? I don't mind helping."

"I hate to ask you—"

He covered the small space between them and clasped her arms, compelling her to look up into his face. "You didn't ask. I volunteered. I don't mind. Scott was a friend. You are a friend."

His words melted some of the cold deep in the marrow of her bones. Emotions she'd held at bay wedged a lump in her throat.

He wrapped his arms around her and drew her close. "It's okay to cry."

She fought the tears back. "I don't like to cry."

"Why?"

It's a sign of weakness, of losing control. Her gymnastics coach's words came back to her. Whenever she had fallen in practice, she was never allowed to shed one tear. After years it had become ingrained in her. But she couldn't tell Jameson that. Instead she murmured, "I just don't."

The steady beat of his heart drummed against her ear. His faint scent surrounded her and brought some consolation to her.

"It's never easy losing a loved one," Jameson finally said, breaking the silence. "No matter the reason for the death."

She remembered the death of his wife at the end of last year. Had he had anyone to help him through his pain? He always seemed so alone. Was he experiencing his own loss again?

Cassie pulled back, their gazes reconnecting. "I know. If you ever want to talk about your wife, I'm a good listener."

Surprise flickered in and out of his eyes. "This isn't about me."

If she pushed back her own sorrow and helped Jameson with his, would it fill the void Scott's death left in her? "This is about losing a loved one, and you lost your wife last year."

He backed away. "I had plenty of time to prepare myself for her death. She was sick for quite some time."

"Can you ever really prepare yourself for a loved one's death?"

He took another step away from her. "How did this conversation suddenly become about me?"

"Have you talked to anyone about your wife dying?" She didn't really need to ask him that question. She knew the answer.

His gaze narrowed, his face frowned. "I need to leave. Let me know if you want me to go with you to Scott's when the police give you the okay."

She understood he was closing the door on any conversation concerning his deceased wife. But still, she saw a flicker of pain in his eyes. "I'll let you know when they call. Mom won't want me to go alone, and I don't think she should go right now."

"Are you going to say anything to your mother about the possibility of Scott being murdered?"

"I could only bring myself to tell her it was an accident. She's been through so much with Scott and her own failing health. I don't want her to know it could have been murder until the police declare that officially. I've asked them not to talk to Mom until they absolutely have to. The detective said he would let me know when."

"I'll make sure I don't say anything, but you may want to moderate the news in case some reporter speculates about the investigation."

She nodded. "I hate to think what this will do to Mom if it is true."

The grief he saw in Cassie's eyes mirrored his own grief for his wife. Maybe if he helped Cassie and her mother through their sorrow, it would ease some of his guilt.

"I'd better go. Call me after you talk to the police." Jameson crossed to the dining room entrance.

Outside in the cool fall air, he paused, trying not to remember the words Liz's father shouted at him that day long ago in the hospital. But he couldn't forget them. They burned into his mind as though the man had branded him with them.

You're responsible for my daughter lying here in this bed.

And he couldn't argue that point. He was responsible.

Sunday afternoon Jameson pulled into the long driveway that led to Scott's apartment above the garage. "So the police have made it official. He was murdered."

"That's what Detective Harrison told me. He was hit with some kind of blunt object. The amount of alcohol in his system was minimal, likely poured in his mouth post-mortem. They are searching the surrounding area to see if anything turns up."

"But they're through with the apartment?"

"Yes and his car is in the garage." On the drive to Savannah, she and Jameson had discussed everything but what had happened to Scott, as though they had mutually decided to avoid the subject for as long as possible. "I called Mrs. Alexander and she told me the key would be under Scott's doormat. She wasn't sure she would be home from church when we arrived."

"Did you tell your mother before you left?"

"No. I will when I get back home. I didn't want to leave right after I told her." Cassie opened the passenger door and climbed from the car.

"Does she know you're coming to Scott's place?"

Cassie rounded the front of the vehicle and halted, facing the garage. "Yes. A neighbor is staying with her until I return home. And our pastor is stopping in to see her after church."

Jameson came to her side, his arm brushing against hers. "Now that I see this in broad daylight, his apartment is pretty secluded."

"Yeah, the way Scott wanted it. I helped him move in. I wish I hadn't."

Jameson fit her hand within his. "That wouldn't have stopped him if he wanted to live here." He gestured toward the structure at the far end of the driveway.

The three-car garage sat at the back of the property, with the entrance to the apartment above it around the back. Large azalea bushes obscured the path in several places. "I could easily see someone lying in wait for Scott."

"But I didn't see any signs of a struggle in his apartment, and I doubt anyone hit him over the head and dragged him up the steps."

Cassie gasped. "You think it was someone Scott knew?"

"Possibly."

The implication sent her heart pounding, its roar drowning out all sounds for a few minutes as she thought of her brother being killed by someone he trusted. A cool breeze stirred the leaves on the live oak shading the driveway, causing the Spanish moss to dance as though someone were pulling its strings. Cassie hugged her sweater to her.

"What do we do?" she whispered around the knot in her throat.

"We check out his apartment and let the police know if anything is missing. Then we let them do their job."

The way he said "we" warmed her. She felt comforted just knowing she wouldn't have to go through this ordeal alone. "Thank you."

"I'm just doing what any friend would do." He guided her toward the stairs.

Slowly Cassie mounted the steps, each one bringing her closer to the murder scene. She withdrew the key from under the mat and tried to unlock the door, but her hands shook.

"Here, I'll do it." After taking the key from her grasp, Jameson inserted it into the keyhole and turned it. He eased the door open, then faced her, taking her quivering hands within his. "I'm with you every step of the way. If you want to do this another day, just say the word and we're out of here."

She welcomed his presence more than he would ever know. She forced herself to smile, but she couldn't maintain it. "I need to get this over with. If something is missing, it might help the police find out who killed Scott."

Wordlessly Jameson entered her brother's apartment first, scanning the living room before allowing her inside. When she stepped through the entrance, she found it difficult to breathe. Her gaze was riveted to the spot on the carpet where Scott had been lying, the dry, red stain ridiculing her remaining composure. The faint stench of blood accosted her nostrils, and she gagged.

She bit her lower lip and backed up, her fingers pressing into her mouth. Suddenly she wanted to cry, but no tears came. Scott was gone. She no longer had to protect him and look out for him, but she wished she still did.

"I don't know how I'm going to tell Mom Scott was murdered."

Jameson drew her past the place on the rug where they had found Scott and down the short hall. "Let's start in his bedroom."

The first thing that struck her when she saw the room was how neat and orderly her brother had always been. Even his bed was made, whereas she often left hers a mess. They had been so different. She stood in the entrance and swept her gaze over the pieces of furniture, trying to visualize what Scott had.

"His TV is still here. And his radio." Cassie walked farther inside, trying to remember what she'd helped him move a few months back. "He really doesn't have a whole lot besides his TV, radio and—" she spun around "—his computer. Did you see it in the living room?"

"No. Where does he usually keep it?"

Cassie crossed to the closet and opened it. "Wherever he decides to work. It's a laptop." After inspecting the contents of the shelf and floor, she turned toward Jameson. "If his murder is connected to his work, then the computer is important as well as his tape recorder."

"Then let's search for them." He made his way back into the living area.

Cassie again paused in the entrance, glad that the couch blocked her view of the red-stained carpet. She did a visual sweep of the large room with the kitchen off to the left, but saw nothing out of place. A picture of her brother sitting at the small kitchen table typing on his laptop popped into her mind. She peered toward it, but its bare surface mocked her.

While Jameson circled the spacious open area, Cassie hung back, frozen in place. Sweat broke out on her forehead and palms. She watched while Jameson opened cabinets and drawers in the small kitchen and even checked the refrigerator.

Finally he faced her, his gaze reaching out to her. "I can't find the laptop or recorder. Would they be anywhere else?"

"Maybe in his car. I know the police inventoried its contents. They didn't say anything about his laptop being in it."

"How about at the paper?"

Cassie shook her head. "He has a computer there. And he always had his recorder on him in case something came up unexpectedly. There wouldn't be any reason for it to be at the newspaper."

"Then let's take a look at his car. If we don't find them, we can tell the police they are missing for sure."

"Which means his murder is probably connected to something he was working on."

Jameson closed the space between them. "Yes. Do you know what story he was writing?"

"No, he always kept things secret until his story came out. The last story published was that series on corruption at nursing homes run by the Bender Corporation. The last article was a few days ago."

"Let's go check his car, then call Detective Harrison."

"Yeah, I need to get home and talk to Mom before someone else tells her." But first she had to walk past that stain in the carpet.

She started forward but couldn't move. When Jameson turned back to her, her gaze shifted toward the area where Scott had been lying when they had found him Friday night. "I—I can't..."

Jameson held out his hand for her.

A fine sheen of perspiration covered her face. She rubbed her damp palms against her jeans, then lifted one toward him. It quavered between them.

His firm clasp surrounded her fingers. "You won't have to come back here again, Cassie, if you don't want to."

His calm voice soothed her raw nerves, but still her legs wouldn't obey the command from her brain to walk.

I can do this.

Then suddenly Psalm 23 flowed through her mind, prodding her forward. When she got to the place where the red stain was, she said out loud, "Even though I walk through the valley of the shadow of death, I will fear no evil, for You are with me."

A few seconds later a chilly breeze whipped her long hair around her face. While Jameson locked the door, she gripped the wooden railing and relished the scent of fall in the fresh air.

Her heartbeat returned to normal as she repeated the last two verses of the Psalm. *Surely goodness and love will follow me all the days of my life, and I will dwell in the house of the Lord forever.* Anything was possible with Jesus by her side, even coping with her brother's murder.

"Are you okay?" Jameson positioned himself on the first step.

When she looked toward him, they were eye to eye, compassion darkening his gaze. Eleven months ago he'd buried his wife. He knew exactly what she was going through. In that moment a connection sprung up between them that went beyond friendship. He felt it, too, she could tell.

He glanced away, scanning the driveway. "Where's Scott's car?"

Cassie gestured toward the garage. "In there. He paid a little extra to park his prize in there."

"Didn't you say he drove a Mustang?" Jameson headed down the stairs.

His speaking of Scott in the past tense caused her to stumble on the last step. She grabbed the railing and steadied herself. She gripped the wood for a few seconds, then pushed away from the stairs while desperately preparing herself to see something Scott had loved.

"Yes, he had to restore it. He'd been working on it for years and finally finished it a few months ago." Cassie led the way to the side entrance into the garage.

"I remember him saying something about it."

Sitting at the far end was the red Mustang. The light streaming through the set of windows in the door reflected the high-gloss polish of the metal and chrome. Memories overwhelmed her—of Scott working on the car, of him searching the junkyards for just the right part.

Jameson whistled. "She's a beauty. What are you going to do with her?"

The question took her by surprise. "I don't know. I can't see anyone else driving the Mustang."

Jameson tried the car door. "It's locked."

"Scott kept a key hidden in here in case he ever lost his other one." Cassie examined the paneling along the back wall and found what she was looking for. She pried a board up and retrieved the second set.

After she tossed Jameson the key, he used it to unlock the car. He stuck his head inside and felt under the front seat. "There's nothing in here. I'll check the trunk, too." A minute later he announced, "They aren't in here, either."

Cassie sagged against the front bumper, her hand

splayed over the shiny red hood. "Then the laptop and recorder were stolen."

"I'll call the police and let them know, then we'd better head back to Magnolia Falls."

An hour later as Jameson pulled up to her house, Cassie hadn't thought anything could be worse than having to check out Scott's apartment. But she was wrong. She still had to tell her mother about her son being murdered. Cassie didn't even know where to begin.

While Jameson climbed from his vehicle, she rested her hand on the handle, watching him come round the front and to her side. Her body was frozen in place. She kept thinking about her mother's poor health and what the news would do to her. She was the only close family her mom had left.

I am with you always to the very end of the age. The verse came unbidden into her mind and comforted her.

Lord, please help me so that I can do this. She yanked on the handle and pushed the door open.

Jameson assisted her from the car and placed his hand at the small of her back as they walked to the porch. Before Cassie had a chance to unlock the front door, it swung open and revealed her neighbor's worried face.

"I'm so glad you're back," Mrs. McVay said. "The phone has been ringing nonstop. I finally took it off the hook, but your mom doesn't know that."

"Who's been calling?"

"Mostly the press. They want a statement about your brother's murder."

Cassie gasped. "I didn't think about that. What did you tell them?"

"Nothing. I hung up, which I'm sure made them call all the more. Thankfully Victoria was taking a nap."

"Is she still asleep?"

The woman shook her head. "I fixed her some tea. She's out on the back porch drinking it."

Cassie hugged her neighbor. "Thanks for everything. I'll take care of it."

"You're welcome, dear. I'd do anything for you and your mom." Mrs. McVay waved goodbye and hurried toward her house.

Cassie walked through the living room and pushed open the swinging door into the kitchen. "A couple of ladies from the church brought over some food right before I left for Savannah." She glanced back at Jameson, who was right behind her, so close she could smell his light scent. "Would you like to join us for dinner?"

"I would hate to intrude—"

"Nonsense, Jameson. Cassie is right. You should stay for dinner. You've been such a big help to us."

Cassie whirled around to find her mother standing at the counter with several casserole dishes in front of her. "Mom! I thought you were out on the porch. Resting."

"I've had my fill of resting, sleeping, doing nothing. I need to stay busy. I'm fixing us something to eat. What would y'all like to have?" Her mother lifted the first lid. "We can have tuna casserole or—" she checked the next dish "—or chicken and rice with broccoli. Which will it be?"

Cassie slid a look toward Jameson next to her. "I don't care. Whatever you want."

"I tell you what, Mrs. Winters. Let me throw something together while you and Cassie talk out on the porch."

"But I—"

"Mom, come on. We haven't had much time today—"

Her mother frowned. "I know when I'm being managed. What aren't you telling me, young lady?"

"I talked with a Savannah detective this morning."

"And he told you Scott was murdered."

Cassie's mouth dropped open. "How did you know?"

"I knew something—" her mother patted her chest over her heart "—was wrong in here. I called Mrs. Alexander after you and Jameson left this afternoon. She told me. Quit trying to protect me. I'm stronger than you think. If you want to talk, I'll be out on the porch." She grabbed the handle and wrenched the door open.

Stunned, Cassie stared at the spot where her mom had been standing only a few seconds before.

Jameson turned the oven on. "Now that Scott's body is going to be released, you probably should talk to her about funeral arrangements. She needs to be a part of that."

"Yes, and I need to call our pastor to see when the church is available." Cassie strode to the wall phone and punched in some numbers.

Jameson listened to her make arrangements for her pastor to come over for dinner. That was his cue to leave. Talk of a funeral stirred memories he wanted to forget of his wife's. Liz's parents had made it clear throughout her funeral what they thought of him. The small, intimate service had lasted an eternity.

As Cassie hung up the phone, Jameson stuck a casserole dish into the oven. "This should be ready to eat in about forty minutes. I'll get everything else laid out for dinner, then leave."

"Leave? Why?"

"Because your meeting with your pastor is a family affair. I don't belong." The last time he had been in a church was his wife's funeral, and before that it had been years. He'd walked away from the Lord when He had abandoned him and Liz.

"I'll call you about the funeral. I hope you'll be a pallbearer. You meant a lot to my brother."

"Sure. Just let me know what I can do."

"I'll call you later about the arrangements, and thanks again for going with me to Scott's apartment. I couldn't have done it alone."

"Under the circumstances, you shouldn't go there alone."

"You don't think we're in danger, do you?"

Jameson leaned against the counter, folding his arms over his chest. "I don't know. Probably not if the killer got what he wanted."

"He has the laptop and the police said Scott didn't have the tape recorder on him. What else…" Cassie's eyes widened as the realization hit her.

Jameson straightened. "What is it?"

"We didn't find Scott's notepad. He used it whenever someone didn't want to be recorded."

FIVE

"Thank you, Jameson, for driving us home this afternoon. I'm so looking forward to spending some time alone with my Bible." Victoria Winters gathered her purse from the floor of the car and set it in her lap.

Jameson threw her a smile as he pulled into the driveway. "I'm glad I could help."

"Cassie, dear, you don't think anyone was upset that I didn't invite them back to the house after the reception at the church?" Mrs. Winters glanced at her daughter in the back seat.

"No, Mom. I'm sure they understood."

"It's just that we've had so much company these past few days."

In the rearview mirror Jameson saw the tired lines around Cassie's eyes, and the urge to comfort her took him by surprise. He'd wanted to do that a lot lately, and he had no business becoming any more involved in Cassie's life than he already was.

He switched off his engine. "I'll help you carry the food inside, then I need to be on my way."

"I didn't mean you, Jameson. Stay and keep Cassie company. After fixing the dinner Sunday night, then leaving, the least you can do is let us return the favor. Stay and eat with us." Mrs. Winters gestured toward the back seat, which was filled with dishes that various members of the congregation had brought to the reception. "We certainly have more food than we could possibly eat in the next few weeks."

He opened his door. "As much as I would love to, I have a class to prepare for."

"Maybe some other time, then." Cassie's mother climbed from the car and came around to help with the food.

Cassie took the plastic container with a chocolate cake from Jameson. "This is going to ruin my diet. All Scott ever talked about was how great Mrs. Alexander's chocolate cakes were."

"I'll take it off your hands if you want." Jameson crossed the grass to the porch.

"Oh, I wouldn't want to be responsible for you gaining any weight. I'll keep it."

Jameson liked hearing Cassie's chuckle. The past few days there had been little of that. He'd seen the worry in her eyes. Scott's notebook never turned up. The police didn't have it, and after a trip back to her brother's apartment, he hadn't found it there, either. Which meant the killer had it. If only he had answered the phone that night instead of leaving town, then maybe he would know what Scott had been working on.

Could he have prevented him from being murdered? That question had haunted him for the past few days.

He held Cassie's cake while she unlocked the front door and pushed it open. He entered last and nearly bumped into her when she came to an abrupt halt inside the living room. She tilted her head to the side and stared at the coffee table, where some magazines were strewn across its surface. Then with a slight shake of her head, she continued on into the kitchen.

After placing the cake on the counter, Cassie scanned the room. Her hairs on her nape tingled. She waited until her mother left, then said to Jameson, "Something's not right."

He set his dishes on the top refrigerator shelf, then turned toward her. "What do you mean?"

She pointed toward the living room. "Those magazines weren't like that when we left the house and—" she walked to the desk near the wall phone "—this chair was pushed all the way in. It wasn't sticking out like this."

"Are you sure? Maybe your mother moved it."

Sure? No, but still… She massaged her fingertips into her temples, trying to think back to earlier that day right before they had left for Scott's funeral. "It doesn't feel right." She pulled the desk drawer out and studied its contents. "I think someone has gone through this. The stacks are wrong. I paid this bill. It should be in that pile." She spun around on her heel, her arms stiff at her sides. "Someone's been in here, searching the house while we were gone. I'm positive."

"Then let's call the police." He reached for the phone.

She held up her hand, saying, "Wait," then she checked the back door. "It's locked. So how did the person get in here?"

"A key? Do you leave one outside for emergencies?"

Her grasp still on the handle, she flattened herself back against the door. "No, but…" Something nagged at her mind. What? If she wasn't so tired and emotionally exhausted, she'd be able to think clearly.

Jameson closed the distance between them. "Did Scott have a key to this house?"

"Yes! He kept it on his key ring."

"Where's the envelope of his belongings the police gave you when they released the body?"

"I put it away. I couldn't open it."

"Go get it. Let's check to see if his keys are there."

Cassie hurried to her bedroom, where she had stashed the manila envelope. After retrieving it, she poked her head into her mother's room to see if she was all right. She lay sleeping on top of her covers, her Bible open beside her.

Back in the kitchen Cassie ripped the package open and dumped its contents on the table. Scott's worn brown billfold, class ring and MP3 player tumbled across the smooth oak surface.

"No keys." Jameson picked up the wallet and opened it, withdrawing a business card stuck where the bills were kept. "In and Out Mart on Peach Street, here in Magnolia Falls."

"I know the place. It's been around forever. Family owned."

"Yeah, I've stopped there a couple of times. It's on the other side of town on the way to Savannah."

"Maybe Scott stopped there the last time he came to town."

Jameson flipped the card over. "There's a phone number on the back."

Cassie snatched up the receiver. "Let's try it. I bet Scott grabbed the card to write it down." She placed a call to the number.

"Brookside Psychiatric Hospital and Clinic. How may I direct your call?"

Psychiatric hospital? Was Scott investigating a story or was he having a relapse? The police still didn't know if Scott had bought the whiskey or if the killer had.

"Hello?"

"Oh, sorry," Cassie hurriedly said, "where are you located?"

After the receptionist gave Cassie an address in Savannah, she thanked the woman and hung up, a headache beginning behind her eyes. "I don't understand. Why would Scott be interested in a psychiatric hospital if he was doing something on the basketball team?"

"Maybe he wasn't. Did he ever talk much about the skeleton found on campus a few months back?"

"He was curious like everyone else, but…" She chewed on her bottom lip. "Do you think he had a lead on who it was or what happened to the woman?"

"That would be the kind of case that would interest an investigative reporter who went to Magnolia College." Jameson walked back to the table and tossed the wallet on it. "If I were still a reporter, I'd be interested."

Cassie slid the billfold toward her and opened it, desperate to find something in it that would lead to the murderer. "Maybe there's something else in here."

"I'm sure the police already checked all this out before giving it back."

Removing all the items in his wallet, she spread them across the table. "Well, we can certainly rule out robbery. He had nearly a hundred dollars in here and not much else." She eyed his driver's license with his picture on it. The pounding in her head intensified as she stared into Scott's solemn gaze.

"He didn't have a credit card?"

"No. But here's his insurance card. I know the police

haven't completely ruled out robbery, but a robber would have at least taken the money."

"I know the detective in charge of the case with the skeleton on campus. Let me call him and have him come over so you can report the break-in."

"I feel kind of silly. I don't think anything was taken and there's nothing obvious that points to someone breaking into the house."

"But your brother's keys are missing with a key to this house on them. That means something."

"Yeah, it means I'm going to have the locks changed."

While Jameson called his friend, Cassie looked up a locksmith. Until she got new locks, she wouldn't feel safe in the house, and now she wasn't even sure she would after that. The thought that someone had come in and carefully gone through their things scared her, and yet she couldn't let her mother see her fear.

"Jim will be here shortly. Maybe he'll tell us where he is with the investigation."

"I don't think they have much. I know Lauren and Dee, my friends, have been involved in a Web site, trying to find all the alumni from ten years ago."

"Any women you know missing?"

"There are some. Do you want something to drink while we wait? I'm getting some iced tea." Her throat parched, she opened the refrigerator and took a blue pitcher out.

"Sure." He went to the cabinet, selected two tall glasses and put them on the counter near Cassie.

The automatic gesture spoke of how familiar Jameson had become with her house after spending the past few days assisting her and her mother with the funeral arrangements. She appreciated all he'd done, couldn't help wondering what had prompted it.

After sitting at the table and taking a sip of her tea, she looked him in the eye. "You don't have to stay, especially if you have something to do. We've taken up so much of your time lately. You've got classes and papers to grade. I can take care of the police."

"I know you can, but I want to stay."

"Why?"

He took his time bringing the glass to his lips and taking a large swallow of his drink. "Because I feel I should have been there for Scott when he called me for help."

"You were out of town. You said you called him when you got back. What more could you have done? None of us could have anticipated what happened to him."

"But I didn't tell you that he had called me as I was getting ready to leave. I let the answering machine take the call."

"Oh. What did Scott say?"

"He wanted to talk to me about the story he was working on. He didn't sound scared or anything. He just sounded like he needed some advice."

"Why didn't you talk to him?"

He averted his gaze for a long moment, and when he looked up, there was a bleak expression in his eyes. "The truth?"

"Always."

"You scare me."

"I do?"

Avoiding looking at her, he wiped the perspiration off the outside of his glass. "You make me feel things I have no right to feel."

Cassie's mouth dropped open, but she quickly snapped it closed before he saw her incredulous expression. She didn't know what to say to his declaration. He made her feel things she'd never felt before, and she wanted to explore what was happening between them. But he obviously didn't. Hurt burrowed deep into her heart.

Silence stretched between them; the only sound heard in the kitchen was the loud ticking of the clock on the wall. The noise grated on her nerves.

Finally she said, "What am I supposed to say to that? You shouldn't feel guilty because you didn't talk to Scott when he first called you? You shouldn't. You didn't know what was going to happen."

"If I had talked to him, I'd at least know what he was working on. I might have even been able to prevent his death."

"How? No one could stop my brother when he was following a lead. He thought he was invincible." The pain behind her eyes increased. She wanted to roll the cold glass across her forehead, but instead she took several gulps of the iced tea. "We don't even know if the piece he was working on was what got him killed. Remember, he's angered a few people with his recent articles." Cassie caught sight of the telephone book lying open to the yellow pages. "I need to call a locksmith."

She shot to her feet and punched in the numbers of the one she'd found earlier. As the phone rang, the doorbell chimed. "Can you get that?"

While Jameson left the kitchen, the locksmith answered and Cassie quickly persuaded the man to come to her house later that afternoon. When she hung up, Jameson returned with a man dressed in a black suit and striped tie.

"This is Detective Jim Anderson of the Magnolia Falls police. Jim, this is Cassie Winters. She's sure someone went through her house while we were at her brother's funeral."

"Scott Winters?"

"Yes, we buried him a few hours ago." If she said the words enough, the reality of Scott being gone might sink in.

"I was so sorry to hear about his death. I'm a big basketball fan and loved seeing him play for the college. It was tragic when he hurt himself in that play-off game."

Her legs weak, Cassie sat again at the table before she collapsed, while Jameson and Jim each took a seat across from her.

The detective removed from an inside coat pocket a small notebook much like the one her brother had used. "What's missing?"

Cassie frowned. "I don't know that anything is missing, at least nothing obvious."

Jim looked around, his gaze fixing upon the back door. "Then how do you know someone broke in?"

"Items weren't where they should be and my brother's key to this house is missing from his effects."

"Are you aware that the Savannah police are investigating his death as a murder?" Jameson asked, leaning back against the counter behind his friend.

"Yes, I'd heard. You think this has something to do with his murder?"

Cassie nodded. "Why else would anyone have broken in and not taken anything?"

"True." The detective jotted something down in his pad. "I'd like you to go through your house, though, and make sure nothing is missing, especially jewelry, silver, small stuff that would be easy to carry."

"I will, but we don't have any valuable jewelry or silver." Her mother had sacrificed everything for her and Scott's sports training.

"Still, you need to check. We have to rule out a simple robbery. Why do you think someone would want to kill your brother?"

"His stories sometimes stepped on certain people's toes."

"And you think that's the case here?"

Cassie ran her hand through her hair. "Maybe. I don't know what to think. All I really know is that Scott is dead." Frustration churned her stomach and tap-danced against her temples.

"What was he working on?"

"We don't know," Jameson answered, his own irritation ringing in his voice. "It could be something that's already appeared in the paper. It could even be about the skeleton found at the college library."

"If he found out anything regarding that, then he found more than we have. We don't even have an ID on the skeleton yet. We know it is a female, probably early twenties, and that she has been in the ground ten years. She had recently been pregnant. We know little that would point to what happened except there was blunt-force trauma to her head."

A picture of her brother's head injury materialized in her mind. The air rushed from her lungs. "Someone hit Scott over the head. The police haven't found the weapon."

"And you think there may be a connection?"

Jameson pushed away from the counter and came to

the table. "Jim, who knows, but Scott's laptop, recorder and notepad are missing. All the key places where he would keep information on a story."

"So he might have been looking into the murder from ten years ago? Anything else?"

"Jameson and I saw Scott interviewing some of the basketball team last week."

Jim wrote *basketball team* down on his paper. "This is the first year we've got a chance to go to the play-offs since Scott was on the team. It doesn't surprise me he would want to do a story on the subject."

But it surprised her. Cassie couldn't forget how much her brother had avoided anything having to do with basketball after his accident. "I don't know. He didn't follow the team these past few years."

The detective's eyebrows rose. "He didn't? Strange. From what I heard, he lived for basketball."

"Not after he was hurt."

Jim flipped his notebook closed. "Tell you what, I'll ask around and see if anyone knows anything about what Scott was working on while you go through the house to see if anything is missing." He stood and withdrew a business card. "Let me know what you find."

Cassie took the card he slid toward her and came to her feet. "I will. I'm changing all the locks. After the locksmith leaves, I'll do a thorough search."

The detective made his way toward the front door. "I'll contact the Savannah police and let them know what's going on."

When the man left, a van pulled up to the curb. As the locksmith with his toolbox walked toward the house, Cassie murmured, "I wish I knew what was going on."

Jameson placed his hands on her shoulders. "So do I.

I'm going to do my own asking around. Some of the basketball players are in my classes. I'll see what I can find out."

"And I'll talk with Dee and Lauren and see who is still missing."

He leaned close to her ear as the locksmith mounted the steps to the porch. "You know Jim wouldn't be too happy if he thought we were investigating on our own."

His warm breath fanned her neck and caused a shiver to cascade through her. "Someone came into my house. I won't feel safe until I find out what's going on."

"And I'm not going to let you do it by yourself."

"Did you find Scott's notebook?" The voice coming through the phone crackled with tension.

The killer gripped the receiver. "No. I needed more time to look."

"It could point to us. Find it!"

"I'll keep an eye on Cassie and Jameson. The mother isn't a threat. They are."

"Man, this place is packed," Dee Owens said, surveying the tables and couches full of students a week later at the Half Joe.

Cassie cradled her large mug of green tea, its warmth chasing away the chill that had clung to her since the day of Scott's murder.

"Why did you want to meet here?" Lauren Owens leaned into the table, pitching her voice low. "It's always so crowded. I'm surprised we even got a table."

Cassie shrugged, not sure herself except that she couldn't forget that evening she'd spent with Jameson at the Half Joe, when she had seen Scott for the last time.

That was when everything started. "I guess I wanted to go down memory lane. It seems to have worked with you and Seth."

Lauren displayed her engagement ring. "I'm doing this a lot lately."

Will I ever show one off to my friends? Cassie immediately thought of Jameson, and his statement about being scared of his feelings for her. *Why doesn't he think he deserves to be happy?*

"You should have to be her sister and listen to her go on and on about Seth and his son," Dee said with a chuckle.

"I'm so glad you two are finally together."

Lauren shook her head when Dee held up a plate of cookies and offered her one. "Although I love talking about Seth and Jacob, I'm pretty sure that isn't the reason you invited Dee and me to join you here. What's going on?"

"You know how sorry we are about Scott's death," Dee added, nibbling on a peanut butter cookie. "I'm doing some PR now for Magnolia College, and since he went here I've had to field some press questions concerning his murder, especially so soon after the skeleton was found. Even though he wasn't killed here, he's one of our own and the town is still reeling from everything that has happened lately."

"That's what I want to talk to y'all about," Cassie said.

"Scott's murder?"

Cassie glanced at Lauren. "Well, no, not exactly. The skeleton found under the library sidewalk."

Dee frowned. "I wish I could forget it."

"You two have been involved with the Web site trying

to locate the missing alumni. Have you discovered anything? Who haven't you found?"

Lauren flipped her long dark hair behind her shoulder. "There are still some women we haven't heard from. A few we have leads on where they are. Josie Skerritt is supposed to be living in Europe, but we haven't tracked her down yet. Also the same for Payton Bell, who was last heard of in Germany."

"Maybe Payton and Josie are together or have run into each other." Dee finished one of the cookies and eyed the last one on the plate. "Don't forget Tamara Landi and Paige Tatum. No one has talked to them in years."

"Didn't Paige marry our senior year?" Cassie took another sip of her tea.

Dee nodded. "She married and divorced Will Blake, then disappeared."

"I don't blame her. I think Will abused her, though she would never say anything." Lauren crossed her feet.

"Where's Will?" Cassie recalled having a class with Will and the looks he would send her even though he was married at the time Paige.

"He owns the In and Out Mart on Peach Street. He bought it not too long ago from the family who ran it for years." Lauren finished her drink. "I saw him in the store a few months back."

Cassie sat up straight. "Will owns the In and Out Mart? Scott had a business card from there the day he was killed."

"Yeah, Will likes to give them out. That day I saw him, he gave me one. He always thought he was the big man on campus and still tries to act that way."

"I'm glad Paige had the courage to get out of that relationship before he really hurt her." Cassie had once seen the bruises on Paige's arms, as if someone had grabbed her really hard.

"Still, I wonder where she is." Lauren pushed her cup away from her.

Dee's forehead puckered in a frown. "Probably as far from here as possible. Will had a temper, and he wasn't too happy about her leaving him."

Lauren pointed to a corner table at the café. "Remember that time he stormed in here and tried to drag her out?"

Cassie winced. "Oh, do I! Jameson stepped in and made Will leave—without Paige." That had been just another reason why Cassie thought Dr. Jameson King was a knight in shining armor, always coming to a damsel's rescue.

"I think that was the last straw for Paige," Dee said, snatching up the last remaining cookie, to which Lauren gave her sister a reproachful look. "Okay, I know I have a weakness for sweets. I'm not as nutritionally minded as you are."

Her younger sister laughed. Turning her attention back to Cassie, Lauren asked, "Why the interest in who's missing?"

"I'm trying to figure out the last story Scott was working on."

Lauren pulled her wallet out of her purse. "He did come talk to me about the Web site a few weeks back, and I gave him a list of who was still missing. We even talked about him writing a feature story on the missing women, asking where they are now."

"Why didn't you tell me this?"

Lauren's eyes grew round. "You didn't ask. Do you think that a story led to his murder?"

Cassie pushed her fingers through her hair. “I don’t know. Maybe.”

“Then why are you looking into it? That could be dangerous.”

Taking a deep breath, Cassie knew she had to confide fully in her friends. “Someone killed my little brother. If I can find anything to help the police, I will. You should know, too, that someone, possibly the same person, searched my mother’s house the day of the funeral.”

Dee glanced around her, then asked in a loud whisper, “He did? What did he take?”

“Nothing. That’s why I think it’s connected to Scott’s murder.”

“What would you have they would want?”

“That’s a very good question, Lauren, and if I had the answer to it, I probably would know who murdered Scott.”

Dee patted Cassie’s hand. “Please be careful. We’ve had enough dead bodies. I don’t want any more, so watch your back.”

“I’ll be careful. And Jameson is helping me.”

“Ah.”

Cassie threw Lauren an exasperated look. “What’s that supposed to mean?”

“I remember that crush you had on him in college. Now that he’s a free man and you’re both adults, I say go for it.”

That’s just it. He isn’t a free man. Cassie kept her thoughts to herself, but she remembered the sadness that lurked beneath his surface. “We’re just friends.”

Lauren chuckled. “Sure.”

If she said it enough, Cassie hoped she could convince herself.

SIX

Sitting in the bleachers, Jameson watched the college basketball players running up and down the court during practice. He noted that Marcus Reed could be a top round pick in the NBA. He was even better than his brother, Kevin. He had the control and precision that Scott had had when he was playing for the team.

Why had Scott been talking to the members of the basketball squad just days before his death? In the break between his afternoon and evening classes, Jameson had decided to drop by the gym and check out the team, hopefully catch a moment to speak with a few players.

It wasn't that unusual for faculty to watch practice. But if anyone asked why he was here, he was prepared to say he wanted to see one of the students he advised. Sam Collins had more potential off the court as a journalist major than on it as a player. They had a good relationship. He decided to start with Sam and see if he could discover what Scott had been after.

At the end of practice, after saying something to Zachary Kirkland, the head coach, Sam jogged over to the bleachers. "Hi, Dr. King. What do you think of our chances this year?"

"Impressive, if everyone remains healthy and injury free."

Sam sat in front of Jameson, twisting around to look up at him. "That's always the problem. Injuries can do a team in."

"Let's hope not this season. You all have had a run of bad luck the past few years."

"Yeah, three, but I feel good about this year."

"It seemed to start with Scott Winters's injury."

Sam scratched his head. "You're right. You know, I talked with him two weeks ago. I was a freshman when he was a senior. I wished I could play like he did, before his injury."

"I was at that game. That was a shame. He was counting on playing professionally."

"And he would have if he hadn't gotten hurt."

"Did he come to see the team practice?"

"No, I ran into him at the Student Union. We ended up getting a cup of coffee and talking. I was kind of surprised at first, because he seemed in a hurry when I ran into him."

Jameson glanced around, then leaned forward. "What did you two talk about? This season?"

"No, and that was kind of strange, too. We talked about the past few. I think he was interested in doing a piece on Marcus Reed. Most of his questions were connected to him."

"Oh, anything in particular?"

"He did wonder if Marcus's brother ever came around to see him at practice." Sam peered behind him, then lowered his voice. "I thought maybe he was having second thoughts about Kevin. I know that after the accident their friendship fell apart. I hated to see that. They were so close at one time. Like brothers."

"Did you tell him where Kevin was?"

Sam shook his head. "I couldn't. I don't even think Marcus knows where his brother is. It's like he dropped off the face of the earth."

It seemed several people had. Something wasn't right. He felt it in his gut. "If you hear anything about Kevin, please let me know. I'm sure that Scott's sister would like to talk to him, close a door on that chapter of her brother's life."

Sam rose. "Sure, Dr. King. By the way, have you graded my report yet?"

"I'm working on it. The class should get it back by next week." If he can squeeze his real job in between trying to solve Scott's murder and keeping Cassie safe. Checking his watch, Jameson came to his feet and descended the bleachers. "I'd better get going. I have a class this evening. It was good talking to you, Sam."

The young man loped across the gym to the men's locker room. Jameson waited until he disappeared through the doorway before making his way toward the exit. Outside he paused, noting how the fading daylight cast shadows across the campus. Then he sensed it.

Someone was watching him.

He pivoted, searching the area. The growing darkness hid any observer, but he knew he was out there watching him. Had he gotten close to something?

He shook off the sensation. As long as Cassie was determined to investigate what Scott had been doing, he would, too. He owed Scott at least that much. After his murder was solved, he would figure out how to get on with his life—without Cassie.

* * *

Cassie walked toward the front of the lecture hall. Good thing she wasn't taking the class for a grade. If she had been, she would probably not pass. She'd only jotted down a few notes, unable to focus on Jameson's lecture. The deep, smooth timbre of his voice had lulled her into a state of daydreaming that instantly reminded her of when she had been an undergraduate at Magnolia College.

She waited until the last student finished talking to Jameson before she came up to him. "I talked with Dee and Lauren today."

As he slipped his wire-rimmed glasses in his pocket, Jameson checked to make sure no one was within earshot, then said, "And I went to basketball practice and had a chat with one of the players whom Scott interviewed."

"Let's go somewhere to compare notes."

He watched the last student file out of the lecture hall. "Not the Half Joe. That's not very private. How about coming back to my apartment?"

Although Cassie knew the invitation was solely practical, she still couldn't stop herself from blushing.

He gathered up his briefcase. "I figured you wouldn't want to go back to your house and have your mother overhear us talking about your brother's murder."

"Your place sounds fine. I'll follow you in my car."

Although Magnolia Falls wasn't a big city, Jameson lived across town from the college. After quite a few turns, they still hadn't arrived. Away from the lights and traffic near the school, Cassie began to notice the same pair of headlights behind her. The driver kept his distance, but every turn they made, the car repeated.

Was someone following them?

Jameson pulled into a parking space in front of a two-story, redbrick apartment building on a residential street. Cassie stopped her car right behind his, then glanced back to see where the pair of headlights were. The street was empty and dark.

After climbing from her car and making sure it was locked, she studied the stretch of asphalt that disappeared into the blackness. "I think someone was following us."

Jameson stood behind her. "I think so, too." He draped his arm over her shoulders and directed her toward the large front door. "I also thought someone was watching me earlier this evening."

"Who?"

"It could have been anyone. I guess it could have even been my imagination, too. I haven't played investigative reporter in years. I may be losing my edge."

The laughter in his voice sounded more strained than merry. "At least you had an edge once. I never did."

"And we need to talk about that." He opened the door for Cassie to go inside the building first. "My apartment is on the second floor." He headed for the stairs.

She couldn't help noticing that he no longer had his arm around her. Obviously outside he had meant it as a protective gesture, which endeared him even more to her. At the top of the landing, she peered down into the lobby, half expecting to see someone below watching them. The foyer was as empty as the street.

"Maybe we are imagining things." She waited while Jameson unlocked his door.

He waved her inside. "That's always one possibility."

"And the other?"

"That we're being followed."

She shrugged off her light jacket and handed it to

Jameson. "If we're being followed, then that means we're on to something."

"But what? Does it concern the skeleton or the basketball team?"

"What if it concerned both?"

Jameson chuckled and proceeded into his living room. "You have a vivid imagination. I may have to come to you when I have writer's block."

Cassie surveyed the large room before her. It had a comfortable, lived-in look, with one long navy-and-maroon-striped couch and two blue leather lounge chairs that complemented the sofa facing them. She would even say it was cozy, nothing like her brother's place had been.

"You spend a lot of time here."

Although she hadn't meant it as a question, he answered, "Yes, when I'm not teaching, I'm writing here."

Cassie sat on the couch, resting her arm on a maroon throw pillow at one end. "How long have you lived here?"

"Since I moved to Magnolia Falls." He stood on the other side of his large wood-and-glass coffee table. "Do you want something to drink?"

"No, I'm fine." Suddenly she was self-conscious of the fact they were alone together. She'd been alone with Jameson before, but this felt different.

He looked around for a moment, then chose the lounge chair near her end of the couch, but with a coffee table between them. "Tell me what Dee and Lauren had to say."

After she gave him a rundown of their conversation, she asked, "What did you discover at practice? Who did you talk to?"

Jameson filled her in on his meeting with Sam. "It was outside the gym I felt someone watching me."

Cassie sat forward, threading her fingers together. "So it was most likely someone connected with the basketball team. Was Marcus Reed there?"

"Yeah."

"What does he look like?"

"Tall, slender, dark hair."

Cassie thought back to the evening she had seen Scott talking with a young man in the Half Joe's parking lot. Was it Marcus? "You wouldn't happen to have a picture of him?"

"No, but I could pull one up on the Internet. Why?"

Cassie described the exchange between Scott and the mystery person at the café. "He was tall, slender with dark hair. It could have been Marcus. If so, neither Scott nor he were happy with the way the conversation was going."

Jameson pushed to his feet. "I'll be right back."

When he walked toward the hallway that must have led to the bedrooms, Cassie collapsed back against the cushion and shut her eyes, images and thoughts swirling around in her mind. Scott could have been working on either story, both of them, or neither one. They weren't really any closer to the truth than they were the day after the murder.

She heard Jameson coming back into the room. She straightened while he approached with a laptop and placed it on the coffee table in front of her. Bending forward, she saw a picture of the young man whom Scott had been talking to that night at the Half Joe.

"It was Marcus."

"Maybe there were hard feelings between them, and he didn't want Scott to do a story on him. After all, Kevin disappeared not long after graduation. There was an ugly altercation between them at a party. Both were drunk and they got into a fight." Jameson closed down his computer. "Rumors were flying around campus about the party and the fight."

"Maybe we should find out exactly what happened at that party."

He sank down beside her and rubbed his hands down his face. "I don't know anyone we could ask."

"I do. Tony Blake was in the same year as Scott and on the basketball team. From what Scott told me about him, he was most likely at any party on campus, if not hosting it. His older brother, Will, went to school with me and now owns the In and Out Mart. He may know where Tony is."

Jameson's eyebrows rose. "You're probably right. I'll pay him a visit."

Cassie placed her hand on his arm. "*We'll* pay him a visit."

He frowned. "I remember Will Blake. From what I know of him he isn't a very nice man. I'd rather you not be around him."

"There you go trying to protect me again." She smiled, warmed by the gesture.

"And what's wrong with that?" Although his frown deepened, a gleam sparkled in his eyes.

"Nothing at all, just as long as you let me accompany you." She angled so she faced him. "I want to make whoever killed Scott pay. I can't let this go unsolved."

He stared down at both of her hands gripping his arm now. When he reestablished eye contact, all traces of his frown were gone and something unidentifiable was in his expression. Concern, yes, but that wasn't all.

"When do you want to pay Will a visit?"

"Can you go tomorrow after I get out of school?"

"Sure. I don't have an afternoon class. I'll come by the high school and pick you up."

Satisfied, she sank back, exhausted from the past week. "Good. I know the Savannah police are investigating Scott's murder, but I think somehow it involves Magnolia Falls."

"If we find out anything, we have to let the Savannah detective know, but I also want to keep Jim informed."

"Why would someone go to such lengths to shut Scott up?"

"People murder for all kinds of reasons—passion, greed, revenge."

"And there are some who like to kill for pleasure."

"I don't think that's what's going on here."

Her heavy eyelids slid close. "Neither do I. This is personal. I'm glad you're helping me."

"So you'll listen to my advice on how to proceed?"

She shifted to look at him. "I'll try, but there are no guarantees."

His chuckles tingled through her. "At least you're honest about ignoring me."

"I could never ignore you," Cassie said before she realized what she had admitted to.

He drew in a breath of air, his eyes flaring.

She sat up straight, deciding relaxing was making her say things she shouldn't. "I mean, I will always listen to what you have to say."

"But not necessarily follow my advice?"

She lifted her shoulders in a shrug. "What can I say? I don't even follow my mom's one hundred percent."

His robust laugh transformed his features, easing the world-weary look that was his usual expression. "Your honesty is so refreshing."

"I don't feel very refreshed." Cassie yawned. "And if I don't leave now, I might fall asleep at the wheel."

She hated to move from the comfortable couch, but that very comfort was luring her to stay longer than she should. Jameson rose and took her hands to pull her to her feet. Eyes locked with hers, he brushed her hair behind her ears. She wanted him to kiss her. Her heartbeat slowed in anticipation. Her stomach fluttered.

One corner of his mouth curved up. "I'll follow you home to make sure you get there all right."

Still so close she could see the lamplight behind the couch reflected in his eyes, she tamped down another yawn and said, "I promise you I won't fall asleep."

Seriousness wiped away his half grin. "I'll feel better if I make sure you get home safely. This isn't up for discussion."

"But…" She started to argue with him, then it dawned on her why he was insisting. "You think the person who followed us earlier is still out there. We may have imagined it."

"I know, but we may not have. I did learn as a reporter to be careful. It saved my life once."

"You are just full of surprises. What happened?"

"An informer turned on me. I did some checking and didn't go to meet him as planned. I found out later it was an ambush."

"My, you've lived an interesting life."

"My life is dull and boring, the way I like it."

There was nothing dull and boring about the man who was inches away from her. He stepped away, retrieving his car keys from his pocket. With regret, she realized the moment was gone.

After donning her jacket, she picked up her purse and searched for her own keys. "I do appreciate the escort home. This cloak-and-dagger stuff isn't my normal routine."

"Which I'm thankful for."

Jameson locked his apartment door and settled his hand at the small of her back as they made their way to their cars.

"Are you working on a mystery?"

"Yep. I will say I never thought I would be involved in a real-life one."

"No one ever is." Cassie opened her car door then faced Jameson.

He started to move away, but closed the small space between them. Cradling her face between his hands, he leaned in and brushed his lips across hers. Softly once, then twice. Legs weak, Cassie nearly collapsed against him but managed to keep herself upright as he deepened the kiss, his fingers sliding into her hair.

All too soon he backed away several feet. She gripped the door to keep herself from sinking to the ground while she tried to calm the rapid beat of her pulse.

His expression hidden by the dark night, he said, "I shouldn't have done that."

Still stunned by his kiss, all she could ask was "Why?"

"Because this—" he pointed to himself, then her "—won't lead anywhere and you deserve a relationship that will."

Shaking the daze from her mind, she straightened. "I meant, why did you kiss me."

"Because I've wanted to all night." He pivoted and strode toward his car.

* * *

"Christiana, have a seat." Cassie sat behind her desk in her small office and examined the beautiful teenager across from her. Her dark eyes reflected anger. "What's wrong?"

Shrugging off her backpack, Christiana plopped down into the chair. "My brother. He will not let me do anything. I have to come home right after school. I cannot go out on a school night. He just does not understand I like to study with my friends."

She'd seen the teenage girl on several occasions since August, most of her complaints directed at her older brother. Edgar Ortiz was trying to take the place of their parents, who had died in Brazil. "Have you told your brother why you want to study with your friends?"

Christiana nodded. "He said he can help me when he gets home from work. He has gotten worse since that skeleton was found on campus. He thinks something like that is going to happen to me."

"Have you thought of trying out for a sport so you'll have something to do after school?"

The teenager slouched in the chair, shaking her head. "I'm not interested, except maybe soccer. But it's too late to try out for the fall season."

"There'll be a spring one."

"When a boy calls, Edgar hangs around while I talk with him. He will not let me date, not even a group one."

"First, continue to talk to him about how you feel. Second, have your friends over to your house. Let him get to know them, then maybe he will feel more comfortable with you going out with the group."

Staring down at her hands clasped together, she mumbled, "He is so strict. He will probably scare away my friends."

"Have you given him a chance?"

The young girl shook her head.

"Try it and see what happens."

The dismissal bell rang. Christiana stood, grabbing her backpack. "I will think about it."

"I know your brother. We went to college together. I'm sure he has your best interest at heart." Cassie rose and rounded her desk. "You know my door is always open. Let me know what happens."

"Thanks, Miss Winters, for listening. Sometimes I get so frustrated...." Her words trailed off into silence. "I had better go or I will miss my ride."

At the door Cassie watched the teenage girl leave and disappear into the flow of students leaving the high school for the day. Christiana Ortiz wasn't the only one without parents, living with a sibling. She'd come to her before, wanting advice that a mother usually gave a daughter. Christiana needed an adult female in her life on a regular basis.

She turned back into her office. She remembered how Scott had struggled in high school without a father figure. Her mother had tried, but there were things that she couldn't do for her son.

Cassie leaned against the edge of her desk. She needed to do something. Maybe she could start a mentoring program at the school. Or maybe she could establish a study group where teens could get help. She could even get Edgar's input at church. If he bought into whatever she came up with, then he might allow Christiana to be a part of the program.

When she saw Jameson coming toward her office, she went to her file cabinet and withdrew her purse. She would have to think about this later.

At the door Jameson studied her for a few seconds. “Are you okay? Something happen?”

“No, I just met with a student who has me thinking about forming some kind of mentoring program or study group.”

“Everyone can use someone to turn to in time of need.”

Cassie slung her purse strap over her shoulder. “Right, especially a confused teenager.”

“Are you ready to go?” Jameson gave her a smile that sent her pulse racing.

“Yes, as ready as I can be. I don’t really relish seeing Will again.”

“Why?”

“I was friends with his wife. I know what he’s capable of.”

“Murder?”

Cassie came to a halt in the hallway. When Jameson turned back to her, she said, “I hate to say it, but yes. You think he could be involved in Scott’s murder?”

“Right now anyone could be.” He walked the few paces back to her. “Maybe you shouldn’t go.”

She hugged her purse close to her. “I’m going. I’m not scared of Will.”

“Maybe you should be. Being scared can keep you safe.”

“But you can’t let it rule your life. Life happens. We can’t always control it.”

“I’m not sure we have much control at all.”

“Sure we do. We choose how we respond to what happens to us.” Suddenly they were talking about something that had nothing to do with Will Blake or Scott’s death.

Jameson began walking again toward the front door. “What happens when you get overwhelmed with life?”

"Like now? My faith sustains me. I pray a lot."

Outside he paused on the top step. "What if you gave up on the Lord helping you?"

"Have you?"

His penetrating gaze seized hers. "I've learned over the years to depend only on myself."

"That sounds very lonely."

He faced forward and descended the stairs. "But not as disappointing."

"All I can say is that the Lord hasn't given up on you. That help you wanted might not have been what was best for you. Maybe He's been there the whole time and you just haven't recognized it."

At his car, Jameson stared at her for a moment. "How did we get on such a heavy topic?"

In other words, he was through with discussing his relationship with God, or more accurately the lack of one. Their connection might not go beyond friendship, but in this she might be able to help Jameson find his way back to the Lord. Although he was good at masking his true feelings most of the time, she'd gotten glimpses of a lonely, hurting man. She wanted so much to help him.

She attempted a smile that she fought to maintain. "I have no idea, but if you want, we can talk about the weather instead."

"Cassie Winters, are you making fun of me?" He ducked into the car.

When she settled into the passenger seat, he started the engine and pulled out into traffic. "Never. Just teasing you."

He glanced at her. "Will you allow me to question Will?"

She mimed zippering her mouth and tossing the key away.

He laughed. "This I've got to see. You being quiet."

Cassie pressed her lips together and remained silent for the rest of the short trip to the In and Out Mart. When she entered the store, there were only a few customers milling around. One young man, probably a student at the college, stood behind the counter.

Jameson headed toward him. "Hi, Sam. I didn't realize you work here."

"Since the beginning of the school year."

"Is Will Blake here?"

"Yes, in his office." Sam waved his hand toward a door at the back of the store.

"Good. We need to talk with him. We'll show ourselves in."

Before the young man could say anything, Jameson grasped Cassie's hand and hurried toward the metal door that led to a short hallway.

A raspy voice that Cassie recognized as Will's could be heard in the corridor, saying, "I told you I would take care of it."

SEVEN

Jameson paused at the door to Will's office. He raised his hand to knock but didn't. Instead, leaning forward, he waited. Right behind him, Cassie pressed near him.

"You've got it. I can cover it," Will said, then they heard the sound of a receiver being slammed down.

The sharp noise followed by a curse caused Cassie to flinch, then to step away. Jameson wished she were anywhere but with him. Whatever possessed him to agree to her accompanying him on this fishing trip? He could almost feel Will's anger pulsating from the office.

He raised his arm to knock on the door when it swung open and Will's glare met his. Some of the fury dissolved as the man realized who was in the hallway.

A neutral expression fell into place. "Dr. King, what are you doing out here?" Will peered past Jameson to Cassie, a slight rounding of his eyes indicating his surprise at seeing her. "Cassie, I was sorry to hear about Scott's death. I wish I could have come to the funeral, but..." He let the rest of his explanation fade into silence.

"May we have a word with you?" Jameson asked, moving into Will's line of vision locked on Cassie.

Will stepped to the side and allowed them to enter. "What do you need?"

Again Jameson wanted to shield Cassie from Will's scrutiny, but she took her place next to him as if she could read his intention. "We were going through some of Scott's possessions and found one of your business cards. What kind of business did you two have?"

Will drew himself up straight, towering over both of them at six feet eight inches. "I've already told a Savannah detective. Nothing. One of my clerks told me he came to see me when I was gone. He must have given him a card." His gaze swept to Cassie. "I didn't really know your brother. I followed him when he played for the school, and I read a couple of his articles in the paper. Sorry I can't be of more help." He pulled open his door and stood next to it. "Now, if you'll excuse me, I'm late for an appointment."

When Cassie came abreast of Will, she asked, "Have you heard from Kevin Reed?"

Will blinked, averting his look. "Not in years."

"How about your brother, Tony? I didn't see him at the funeral, either. He lives here, doesn't he?"

Will stiffened. "No, Savannah, and I believe he was out of town on business when Scott died, as was I."

"Is he back now?"

"On vacation for two weeks."

"Well, good day, then. Thanks for your—help." Cassie walked into the corridor.

As Jameson came out of Will's office, a door to the left of it opened.

Will moved in front of it. "Good day, Cassie, Dr. King."

The door closed, a soft click sounding in the sudden quiet.

The whole way down the short hallway Cassie could

feel Will's glare burning a hole in her back. When she finally was outside the store, she inhaled several deep breaths of the cool air.

At his vehicle, Jameson grasped her arm and swung her around. "What in the world were you doing back there? What part of 'let me handle the interview' do you not understand?"

His fury blasted her in the face. She flattened back against the side of his car. "I never told you I wouldn't say something. He was lying."

"You think! Of course he was lying." Jameson reached around her and yanked open the door. "Get in. I hope you can at least do that for me." He stalked around the front of the car and slid behind the wheel. "I'm taking you home."

"My car's at the school."

"Then I'm taking you there." He backed out of the parking space.

The drive to the high school took fifteen long, silent minutes in which Cassie tried to think of something to say to the man beside her. The air vibrated with his anger, all directed at her.

When he pulled up next to her car, she finally said, "We need to talk about this."

He glared at her. "No, we don't. I can't do this anymore. I thought I could help you, but not when you carelessly put yourself in danger. I won't be responsible for something bad happening to you."

Shaking but trying to remain calm, she said, "Then you better help me, because I won't stop looking into Scott's death until I have answers."

His knuckles white as he gripped the steering wheel, he stared out the windshield.

The silence ate into any common sense she had. "We needed to know what he knew about Kevin and Tony."

Jameson blew a harsh breath out and turned toward her. "If you had waited before saying anything, you would have realized I was getting around to inquiring about both of them. I wasn't going to leave there without broaching the subject, even if he was insisting we leave."

One part of her bristled at the almost calm, too patient voice he used, as if she were a child he needed to explain something to; the other was amazed at how he could pull himself together so quickly. "Then perhaps you need to clue me in on what you're doing. That's what partners do."

"Partners!"

The abrasive laugh, almost a taunt, that accompanied the one word dangled between them. He wasn't as together as she thought. Now that she really looked into his eyes, she saw his fury seething beneath the surface.

"Then what are we?" Notching her chin up an inch, she threw the challenge into his face.

He opened his mouth to reply, then snapped it close. A nerve in his jaw twitched. "I don't know."

"I appreciate you being concerned about me, especially with Will. He's not a nice person and—"

"That's putting it—"

She held up her hand. "Please let me finish. I will stay away from him if you help me. We got the information we needed from him."

His eyebrows shot up. "We did?"

"He's lying, which means he knows where at least one of them is. We need to dig into his life, maybe follow him until he leads us to either Kevin or Tony."

He shook his head. "You watch too much TV. When

do you want to do this tailing you think will lead us to them? After school from say four to midnight?"

"Okay. Do you have a better suggestion?"

"I'll question Sam, the young man at the counter, and see what he knows. Maybe Kevin or Tony has come into the store. Staking out Will and the market should be the last thing we do. I'm not even sure Will is a good lead to what happened to your brother."

Cassie sighed. "Yeah, I know, especially if Scott was investigating a ten-year-old murder."

"But on the other hand, didn't you say Will's ex-wife is one of the missing alumni?"

"Yes, Paige hasn't been heard from."

"Also, I want to know what was going on in that room next to his office."

"That man certainly shut the door fast when he saw us in the hall."

"Not an action of an innocent person."

She leaned toward him, stopping short of putting her hand on his arm, although the urge was strong to do just that. "You see, if we talk this out and plan we can work as a team."

He locked gazes with her. "I will walk away from this investigation next time if you put yourself in danger. I would never forgive myself if something happened to you."

Maybe she should back off the investigation. Who was she to think she could solve a murder case? All she knew about investigations came from watching TV shows, as Jameson had pointed out. Not exactly the best education.

"What do you suggest we do next?" she asked, still mulling over whether to go any deeper into the case. She needed to pray about it before she made a decision.

"I'm going to talk with Sam. Let's see what he says."

"And there is the psychiatric hospital we could check into."

"We'll probably need to go on Saturday since it's in Savannah. That'll give me time to see Sam."

She opened her door. "Okay. Saturday it is. Call me after you've talked with Sam and we can set a time for our trip."

Jameson watched as Cassie got into her car and started the engine. He let her pull out of the parking lot before him. Spying his trembling hands, he fisted them. A storm still raged inside him. He didn't know how he was going to protect her if she went off on her own. She didn't think she was stubborn, but she had a good dose of it. It was going to drive him crazy.

Memories of twelve years before flooded him. Memories he had run from and could never escape. It had been his job as an investigative reporter that had cost his wife her life. Someone had tried to murder him and instead had gotten Liz. He'd barely survived that guilt. How would he cope if something happened to Cassie? He couldn't allow a second woman to die because of him. Somehow he would keep Cassie safe.

Jameson waited outside the gym after practice as the basketball players streamed out of the building. He followed Sam from a distance until he was alone. Then Jameson approached his student.

"Sam, I need to talk to you. Do you have a few minutes?"

The young man wheeled around, the Gothic facade of the library looming behind him. "Sure, Dr. King. Whatcha need?"

"Some information." Jameson pointed toward a bench set off to the side of the entrance, hidden from view by the azalea bushes.

"Shoot." Sam folded his long length on the bench.

Jameson opened a folder and withdrew a photo of Kevin. "Have you ever seen this man at the In and Out Mart?"

The young man studied the picture. "No, not in person. I've seen a photograph of him in the gym lobby with one of the past basketball teams. Isn't he Marcus's brother?"

"Yes. You've never seen him around? He's never come to see Marcus?"

"I don't think so."

"If you do see him, give me a call right away." Jameson gave Sam his card with his cell number on it. "I know this is unusual, but it's important I talk with Kevin."

"What's this about?"

"I wish I could say, but the less you know the better."

Sam whistled. "I know you used to be a reporter. Are you going to give up teaching to do it again?"

Jameson chuckled. "No. I teach and write books. I don't want another job."

"Ah, is this for one of your stories?"

Jameson didn't answer the question. Instead, he pulled out a second photo and showed it to Sam. "Have you seen this person around the store? Or for that matter, anywhere in Magnolia Falls?"

"That's the boss's brother, Tony. Sure. He comes around about once a week. Goes in the back to speak to Mr. Blake, then leaves. He doesn't stay too long. You know what I think? He comes to get money from his brother, because he's pretty regular about his visits."

"Will you call me when he shows up at the market next time?"

"Sure. If I help you with your book, would you put me in the dedication?"

"I would."

Sam rose, grinning. "Let me know when the book comes out."

As the young man started to walk away, Jameson said, "Sam, please don't say anything to anyone. I don't want people to know what I'm working on."

"Sure, Dr. King. See you in class."

Jameson hated misleading the boy, but he didn't want Sam to get involved. If he knew what he was doing, he could see Sam wanting a more active role in the investigation. He'd always been interested in the investigative part of reporting. One person was dead. He didn't want another person to follow Scott.

Victoria Winters clicked off the cordless phone and laid it on the wrought-iron table. "What's going on, Cassie? That's the third hang-up in the past week, and the number is blocked by caller ID. We never get hang-ups."

Leaning against the railing of the back porch, Cassie faced the yard, cradling a cup of tea in her hands. "It could be a student at school. You know how they like to play pranks. Let me answer next time."

"After what occurred with Scott, I don't like it."

The trace of fear in her mother's voice mirrored how she felt inside, but she didn't want her mother to know. She had enough to worry about without being concerned something might happen to her only remaining child. Cassie hoped and prayed it was a student. But in her gut she didn't think it was.

"When's that nice Dr. King coming to pick you up?"

Cassie checked her watch. "In a few minutes. I'll probably be gone most of the day."

"Are you going to drive Scott's car back today?"

"Yes. I'll try to put most of his things in it."

"Are you sure you don't want me to come with you?"

Cassie turned her back on the yard, sipping her tea. "Do you want to—really?"

Tears filled her mother's eyes. She peered down at the phone near her hand. "No, if I was being truthful with you. I haven't been feeling too well lately."

Cassie came to her mother, put her cup on the glass top and knelt in front of her. "Is Mrs. McVay coming over soon?"

A tear streaked down her mother's cheek. "I don't know why you insist on her keeping me company while you're gone."

"Because you haven't been feeling well. I won't be in town. I couldn't get here fast if something happened to you." Cassie held her mom's hands. "Please, it will make me feel better. Besides, aren't you showing her how to scrapbook?"

A smile pushed through the sad expression. "Yeah. We're about halfway through one for her daughter. She wants to give it to her for Christmas."

"I'm sure Alicia will love the scrapbook if you are involved in it. I love the one you did for me. I'll always treasure it."

"I never got Scott's finished." The tears returned, coursing down her mom's face. "I wanted to put more of his articles in it. I was thinking about giving it to him for his birthday next spring."

Cassie brushed away the wet tracks. "Finish it for you.

I'm sure there will be items in his apartment you can use. When you feel better, you can go through the boxes."

"I don't know, honey. I'm not sure I can."

"I thought I'd have Jameson help me lug them up to the attic. When you're ready, we can get them down." Cassie pushed to her feet, patting her mother's hands. "Give it time."

Door chimes resounded through the house. "That must be your young man. Don't keep him waiting. Your dad always hated it when I made him late."

Cassie bent down and kissed her mom's cheek, then hurried into the kitchen and through the living room to the foyer. When she opened the door, Jameson filled the entrance. Right behind him was Mrs. McVay with a pan of brownies. He let the neighbor enter the house first.

Jameson inhaled deeply. "Mmm. I think those brownies are still hot."

Mrs. McVay paused and peered back at him. "Straight out of the oven. That's why I'm wearing hot pads. I'll cut these up and put a couple in foil for y'all to enjoy on the drive to Savannah."

"A woman after my heart." Jameson closed the door behind him, then followed her neighbor into the kitchen.

So all she had to do was learn to bake like Mrs. McVay and she might have a chance at capturing his heart. Cassie trailed after the pair and waited by the entrance while Jameson got his brownies.

When he turned to her with his prize, his boyish smile made her nervous all over again. "Are you ready to leave?"

He nodded. "You?"

"I was ready when I opened the front door."

"Thanks, Mrs. McVay, for sharing these." He kissed the woman's cheek.

He had a way with women, and Cassie didn't think he was even aware of it. His love for his deceased wife must have been so great. Would she ever experience that kind of love?

Not if she kept pining for a man who could never care for her like that.

Fifteen minutes later she was ensconced in the passenger seat of Jameson's car on the highway to Savannah. The scent of chocolate permeated the small confines, making her stomach growl. She should have eaten breakfast.

"What did Sam have to say?"

"He's never seen Kevin, but Tony comes in once a week. He'll call me the next time he does."

Cassie thought about the hang-up that morning. "Someone's calling and hanging up when Mom answers."

"Has it happened to you?"

"No, but she usually is the one who answers the phone."

"You think it's connected to our investigation?"

She shrugged. "I don't know what to think. Why would someone do that? A kid, maybe, but..." She hooked her hair behind her ear. "I really don't know what to expect. I've never done something like this before."

"Someone could be trying to scare you, or find out if you are at home."

"Well, guess what? I'm scared now. I want it to be one of my students. That I can deal with."

"And it may be. Why don't I have Jim put a trace on your phone. That way we'll know where the calls are coming from."

She fluttered her hand in the air. "Fine. Whatever it takes to make it end. It's upsetting Mom, and she doesn't need that right now. I'm so glad Mrs. McVay is staying with her today."

"Are you going to be okay cleaning out Scott's apartment?"

"No, but it has to be done. It's been several weeks, and Mrs. Alexander has been so patient. I know she has gotten rid of the carpet so I won't have to see the..." She couldn't bring herself to say *bloodstain.* The memory was enough for her to have to handle. She dreamed about it every night.

"So it should be easier, then?"

"I'm not sure easier, but I'll manage. I don't want a stranger going through Scott's things. I already feel like the killer did." Suddenly chilled, she pressed her folded arms to her chest.

"How about the furniture?"

"Most of it is Mrs. Alexander's."

"So we get his personal stuff and the car and bring it back to Magnolia Falls?"

"Yes. Too bad it isn't as easy as it sounds."

"First, our visit to the hospital, then the apartment. After that I'm taking you out to eat."

Something to look forward to in an otherwise awful day. In the forty-five minutes to the psychiatric hospital, Cassie gathered her composure for a very trying day.

At the reception desk Jameson grinned at the young lady manning it. "Good morning. I'm here to visit Kevin Reed. My sister and I are passing through Savannah and wanted to stop by and see our friend." He stepped closer and widened his smile, his full attention on the receptionist. "Can you help me?"

It took all of her willpower to keep from chuckling at Jameson's performance. Most of the time he seemed so unaware of his appeal, but when he needed it, he could use it. The woman beamed as she checked her computer monitor.

"Oh, I'm so sorry. He's no longer with us. He checked himself out three weeks ago today."

Jameson lounged against the desk. "I went by his place before coming here and it looked deserted. That's why I thought he was back in the hospital."

The receptionist adjusted her black glasses that had slipped slightly, then tilted her head, her gaze fixed on Jameson. "Where did you go?"

He gave the young lady Scott's old address.

The woman's mouth puckered in a tiny frown. "He must have moved. That's not the address we have."

Jameson leaned across the desk as though he were going to impart a secret. "What address do you have?"

The lady shifted her adoring look from the screen to Jameson, her frown deepening. "I'm so sorry, I can't—"

Cassie began to cough as if she had swallowed wrong. Her eyes watered and she bent over, trying to get a breath.

The woman shot to her feet and came around the desk. "Can I help?"

"Wa—" Cassie gave another series of coughs "—water."

A few seconds later Jameson came to Cassie's side and patted her back. "Where can I get some water?"

"I'll get it." Flustered, the woman looked around the lobby as though she forget where she could get something to drink. Her gaze lit upon a door off to the side, then back to her desk. "I'm not—"

Cassie waved her silent, drawing in shallow breaths.

"I'm—" she took a deeper gulp of air "—better now. I've got some in the car."

Jameson slung his arm around Cassie as though consoling her, then glanced over his shoulder at the receptionist. "I really appreciate your help. Thanks."

Charm oozed from him, and Cassie clamped her lips together to keep from making a teasing comment.

Outside in the parking lot by his car, she finally laughed. "You must have been a great reporter, at least if the person you were interviewing was female."

"Are you all right?"

"Now you're concerned? I noticed the woman got to me first."

His eyes danced with amusement. "I had to get Kevin's address first."

"Is that a reporter's motto? Get the lead, then check to make sure a friend isn't choking."

He opened her door. "You weren't. Your acting skills aren't too bad. For a second you had me convinced, but then I realized the timing was just too convenient. Quick thinking on your part."

"I had to do something and that's all I could come up with," she said when he came around and got into the car. "Why the brother-and-sister act?"

"I find women are more responsive if they think you might be available."

"So you are aware of your effect on the female population?"

"I'd have to be dead not to see it. I thought the best way to deal with students' advances was to ignore them. And I was married."

"But that's no longer the issue."

After starting the car, he threw her a penetrating look. "Students will always be off-limits to me."

Cassie's gaze fastened onto Jameson's left hand on the steering wheel. The gold band on his finger glittered in the sunlight. "Not all professors have felt that way. When I was in school, there were a couple of rumors flying around the campus, some even involving people I knew."

He backed out of his parking space and turned left at the entrance. "Well, this one won't change."

Their conversation reinforced two things in Cassie's mind. Jameson was still very much in love with his wife and he was a man of integrity. She could remember the first year she was at the college seeing him at her old church. By the third year he'd stopped coming. What happened to change his mind about the Lord? His wife's illness?

Jameson entered an address in his GPS system in his car then began following the directions. "I wonder why Kevin checked himself out of the hospital."

"The same day Scott was murdered. Do you think he had something to do with it?"

"There was no love lost between them by the time they graduated."

"But murder? Kevin used to hang out at our house. Some vacations he stayed in Magnolia Falls with Scott instead of going home. Mom thought of him as a second son."

"People change all the time." His jaded tone pervaded the car.

"That's one reason my faith is so important to me. God doesn't. He's my stability in a world that's constantly changing." She scanned the area of town they were in. Small homes, neatly kept up, graced either side of the street. "Why did you stop going to the chapel on campus?"

He shrugged. "People change. I changed."

"Why?" Cassie asked, surprised at her boldness, but she wasn't going to back down. She wanted to know this man beside her. She wanted to help him as he was helping her.

His jaw hardened. "I spent most of my weekends at the sanatorium with my wife."

"Is that why you gave up on the Lord? Your wife's illness?"

He snorted. "Illness? She was there because of me."

EIGHT

"What happened to your wife?" Cassie shifted around toward Jameson, who pulled to the curb in front of an empty lot.

He looked out the side window. "We're here. This is where Kevin lives."

She leaned forward to peer around him. "But there's nothing here."

"Exactly. He must have given them a false address."

"This isn't going to be easy, is it?"

His gaze swiveled back to hers. "No. The question is, why did Kevin feel he had to give the hospital the wrong address?"

"He was scared?"

"My thought, too. He needed to hide from someone."

"Scott or the person who killed him?"

"It could be someone not connected to either one."

Cassie massaged her temples. "I'm getting a headache from all this."

Jameson put the car into Drive and pulled away. "This won't be the only dead end we run into. Time to take care of your brother's apartment. At least we know that Kevin was in Savannah until three weeks ago."

"I wonder why he was at that hospital."

"I did some checking on it. One of their specialties is helping people recover from substance abuse."

"I wouldn't be surprised. Both Scott and Kevin fell apart after that last game. I think Kevin blamed himself as much as Scott did for the accident that occurred on the court."

Did the same thing happen with you? Cassie wanted to ask Jameson, but he had shut the door on that conversation. If she did her own checking, would she discover the truth about Jameson and his wife's death? Did she want to know? What kind of relationship could they have if he didn't trust her enough to share that part of his life with her?

Twenty minutes later Jameson parked in the driveway at Scott's apartment. When Cassie climbed from the car, she stared at the partially hidden path to the back stairs. She knew that if Jameson hadn't come with her she couldn't have done this, even in broad daylight. The shadows created by the large live oaks seemed sinister. The quiet gave her an eerie sensation. The high wooden fence surrounding the yard lent an air of seclusion to the property that Scott had always craved and that very seclusion had made it possible for him to be murdered without anyone seeing.

Jameson unlatched his trunk and withdrew stacks of folded boxes. "Are you ready?"

I can do this. The Lord is always with me.

Cassie took part of his load and started up the steps. The closer she came to the landing the more she trembled. At the top, the boxes slipped from her grasp and fell to her feet. She stared at the door, unable to move to unlock it.

"You want Mrs. Alexander to pack up? She did offer."

Jameson's deep, soothing voice reached her ears, drawing her full attention to him. The empathy in his expression touched her, and she didn't feel alone.

She shook her head. "I have to. Finding Scott's murderer is the last thing I can do for him. There may be something inside that everyone has overlooked. I knew my brother better than most people. If anyone can figure it out, it will be me." *I hope,* she silently added, and stuck the key into the lock.

When the door swung open, she bent over and scooped the cardboard pieces up into her arms and entered his apartment. The first thing that struck her was the smell of pine and the outdoors. Mrs. Alexander had been hard at work, cleaning the place and airing it out.

Looking around, she saw no evidence a murder had taken place in the apartment. The bloodstained rug had been removed and a new one in various shades of brown was spread across the floor. Her gaze remained glued to the spot where she'd found Scott, and she heard Jameson move inside and put the stack he held down.

A lump lodged in her throat as a barrage of memories flashed through her mind. Scott laughing at one of her jokes. Scott smiling at her when she finished one of her gymnastics routines. Scott crying when he realized he couldn't play basketball anymore. Scott so drunk he couldn't sit up.

Jameson clasped her upper arms from behind and whispered against her neck, "Time does make it more bearable. I promise."

She turned slowly and laid her hand alongside his jaw. "I'm not the only one here hurting. When you're ready to talk about your wife, I'm a good listener."

He started to pull away, but she settled her other hand on his shoulder to keep him there.

"Who laid down the ground rules? Do you think I've forgotten the question I asked you in your car that you ignored? You will never be happy until you come to terms with what happened all those years ago."

He jerked free. "I don't deserve that happiness you talk about. I should have died that day my wife was hurt."

"But you didn't. You denying yourself a full life will not bring her back."

He snagged a piece of cardboard and began to assemble the box. "Don't turn the tables on me. Today is about Scott."

"And that is why I'm saying this to you. I watched my brother almost self-destruct because he couldn't deal with his past."

Jameson tore off some tape and stuck it on the flaps of the box. "And I suppose the next thing you're going to tell me is that his faith was what finally pulled him out of his black hole."

"No, like you, he was angry at God for what happened to him. But after he hit rock bottom and started his slow climb up, it was his faith that kept him on the right path. His AA meetings were at a church. Soon he started attending more than the meetings, and when he found himself wanting to slip back into the hole, he read his Bible and prayed."

"I prayed. God wasn't listening."

"He's always listening. He just may not be answering the way you want."

Jameson started making another box. "We have a lot of work ahead of us."

Frustrated, Cassie snatched up the first one he had put

together and marched toward the bedroom. *Lord, I'm not doing a very good job. I need Your help. How do I reach Jameson and make him see how much he's missing without You in his life?*

"It felt so strange driving Scott's car back to Magnolia Falls." Cassie took the last box out of the back and stacked it against the garage wall where the other ones were. Later they could move them to the attic.

"It's a beauty." Jameson placed his armload down next to Cassie's, then stood back to admire the 1966 Mustang. "I remember my dad had one of these for a few years. He loved that car. Someone hit him and totaled it. He suffered a broken arm and leg, but at least he survived the wreck."

Cassie lounged against the red fender. "Did he get another one?"

"Nope. After that he always bought clunkers. He told me he never wanted to be beholden to a possession like that again. They weren't what was important." Jameson circled around to the trunk and closed it.

"What was important to your father?"

He didn't say anything for a long moment, and then he finally muttered in a tight voice, "God and family, in that order."

"I wish I had known mine. He left my mother when she became pregnant with Scott. I was five. I hardly remember him."

"He didn't keep in touch?"

"He didn't want to have anything to do with a family, especially children. For years I thought I was the reason he walked out on Mom."

"But you don't now?" His gaze linked with hers.

She released a long breath, pushing off from the fender.

"Most of the time I don't, but I supposed there's still a little part of me that wonders if I was the cause of him not wanting children in his life."

Jameson rounded the car and stopped in front of her. "I'm sorry. Thankfully my sister and I always knew we were loved. Life wasn't easy. We grew up in a pretty rough part of Chicago. But we knew where we stood with our parents."

"Scott and I never lacked love. Our mother made sure of that, but that doesn't stop a kid from wondering what life would be like with two parents. She is someone I can look up to with her quiet strength."

"Even when my dad finally got a good job, he stayed in the old neighborhood partially because he was so involved in the church there and partially because he wanted to give back to the community. He was the reason I wanted to change the world. I wanted to root out the bad guys who preyed on the weak."

"Why an investigative reporter and not a police officer or a prosecutor?"

He chuckled. "Believe it or not, I wasn't very good on the debate team in high school, so I couldn't see myself as a lawyer. And I don't like guns, so being a cop was out of the question. But I did like a good puzzle."

She didn't want the evening to end even though she was exhausted emotionally and physically from the long day. "How about something to drink, and if I know my mother, there are some brownies left for us."

"How can I refuse—good company and chocolate?"

She whirled around and tossed a smile over her shoulder. "Exactly. That's why I used the brownies as a lure."

His laughter followed her out of the garage. She

crossed to the porch steps, then waited for him to shut the door. As he strode toward her, the security light illuminated his handsome face. His gaze remained fixed on her the whole way across the yard. Goose bumps spread down her arms from the intensity in his eyes. It seemed an eternity before he was at her side.

"I think summer has decided to revisit Magnolia Falls," she said as she mounted the stairs.

She lifted her gaze toward the sky, clear with a few visible stars shining. The moon hovered above the line of pine trees along the fence. The warm air encased her in nature's perfumed fragrance.

"Winters are never bad compared to the ones we used to have in New York and Chicago."

Inside the kitchen Cassie went to the refrigerator and removed a pitcher of lemonade. "Is this all right?"

"Sure."

The sound of voices from the dining room floated to Cassie. "Mom loves a good board game. I'm glad the pastor and his wife came over, so we didn't need to rush back here."

Jameson grabbed the plate of brownies. "Let's eat these out on the porch. We need to enjoy the perfect fall evening."

She finished pouring two glasses full of lemonade, then made her way outside. She was glad she was alone with Jameson, but she wondered if it was the mention of the pastor that had prompted the suggestion.

In order to see the stars better, she switched off the backyard light before taking a seat on the porch steps. Leaning back against one, she angled herself so she could look at Jameson. He put the plate between them on the top stair.

As her eyes adjusted to the dimness, she saw his on her. One of the things she liked about him was he gave people his full attention when he was with them. She had told him she was a good listener, but she could take lessons from him.

He took a brownie and bit into it. "Mmm. This is wonderful. I'm going to have to get to know Mrs. McVay or pay her to make some for me."

"Knowing her, she would do it for free." She grabbed one for herself. "I'm not a great cook, but I do prepare a mean batch of fudge."

"Oh, a woman after my heart."

Although he said it teasingly, Cassie halted the brownie halfway to her mouth and looked at him. "When all this with Scott is over with, where does that leave us?" The bold question caused her heart to pound painfully slow.

He popped the last bite of his treat into his mouth, then stretched his legs out in front of him and propped his elbows on the top step behind him. He stared out into the backyard. "I don't know. My life has been on hold for so long, I don't know anything else." His attention returned to her. "I'm not going to deny any longer that I care for you, Cassie."

Her heart went from beating slowly to speeding at a dizzying rate. "You're special to me, too."

"But—" he paused, sitting up straight "—I'm not sure I can ever commit to another, and you deserve only the best."

She didn't know what to say to that. She surged to her feet and descended the stairs, then faced him. "I appreciate your honesty. That's one of the reasons I like you so much. If friendship is all you can give me, then so be it." Somehow she would make it work because he needed a good friend, and she couldn't turn away from him. The Lord brought him back into her life, and she would have to place her trust in that.

A light breeze kicked up, bringing with it the scent of roses from Mrs. McVay's garden next door. She remembered Scott helping her neighbor plant the bushes. Her brother had always liked working outside in the garden. The thought sparked an idea. "What do you think about a memorial garden for Scott at Magnolia College? The garden was torn up when the college started construction on the library renovation."

"I believe they have plans to put something in in the spring."

"Yeah, Steff said something about that when I saw her last week. Maybe I could do something in Scott's memory. When I have the time, I love to garden. So did my brother."

"I say go for it." Jameson took another brownie.

"She said they have some of the azalea bushes from when Trevor removed them at the beginning of the renovation. I could use those and buy some other plants for right now, and then in the spring add some more. Fall is a good time to plant some bulbs, too." Cassie picked up her lemonade and drank the sweetly tart liquid.

"When are you thinking about starting it?"

"I'm off Friday afternoon. I thought I would do some then and finish up on Saturday." A strand of her hair whipped across her face. She pushed it behind her ear. "Are you busy on Saturday?"

"Is this your indirect way of asking me to help you with the garden?" Jameson asked with a chuckle.

"Yep. I'm going to recruit a few high schoolers, but I can always use an extra pair of hands."

"I think I can even help out Friday afternoon. I don't have any classes then."

"Maybe by then we could figure out where to go with Scott's investigation."

"Don't say that too loudly. If Jim heard us say that, he'd tell us to leave the police work to the police."

Cassie took another long sip of her lemonade. "I've never been good about minding my own business."

"I've been telling you for years you'd make a good reporter."

"Are you telling me I'm nosy?"

He threw back his head and laughed. "No way am I going to answer that."

"Seriously, what should we do now? We checked out the In and Out Mart and the hospital. Neither place produced another lead."

"Yet. Sam might call me about Tony, and I'm going to do some checking on the whereabouts of Kevin. He may still be in the area."

"So you think we should wait and see?"

He nodded.

"I'm not very good at that, but since we don't really have a choice, I guess I'd better learn how. What about the trace on my phone? Should I call Jim since he'll need my permission?"

"I'll give him a heads-up tomorrow. Get in touch with him on Monday."

"I'm not sure if I want it to be the killer trying to frighten us or one of my students playing a prank."

"Safer if it's a student."

"But if it's the killer, we could get him."

"I doubt he would be calling to you from his own phone."

Her shoulders sagged. "Yeah, I know. It would be just so much easier if there was a sign pointing to the culprit."

"I'm sure the police would like that, too."

Jameson stood, picking up the empty plate and his glass. "Those brownies hit the spot. Sad to say I could have eaten another one."

"You really are a chocoholic. If I'd realized that when I was in your class, I could have bribed you with a whole batch of fudge."

"Feel free to do that, anyway." He turned to go up the steps.

Cassie trailed after him into the kitchen. "Reverend Rogers and his wife must have left. It's so quiet."

Jameson glanced at the clock on the wall. "It's later than I thought. I'd better go."

Cassie walked him to the foyer, noticing indeed her mother had retired for the evening.

At the front door, Cassie held it open and said, "Thanks, Jameson, for making today easier."

He cocked a grin. "My fee is a ride in the Mustang. It'll bring back memories of my childhood driving around with my dad."

"It's a date. How about after we work on the garden next Saturday?"

"Sure."

When he didn't move to leave, Cassie asked, "Is there something else?"

"I'm just waiting for you to close and lock the door, then I'll leave."

"I don't think there's anyone hiding on the porch," she said with amusement.

"Humor me. I'll feel better knowing you're secured behind a locked door."

"Okay."

Jameson waited until he heard the lock click into place before strolling toward his car. When Cassie had said "It's a date," his pulse rate had accelerated. He'd wanted to say, "No, I don't date." Then he realized he was already involved with her whether he wanted to be or not. The thought frightened him. How could he live with himself if something happened to Cassie?

"Dr. King, you wanted me to call if Tony showed up here at the mart." Sam's whispered voice barely carried over the phone line.

"I'll be right there."

"He arrived a moment ago."

"What's he driving?"

"An old blue Chevy truck. It's parked in the back."

"Thanks." Jameson hung up and looked at the student sitting across from him in his office. "I hate to cut this meeting short, but an emergency has come up that I must see to."

The young lady rose. "I appreciate your help. I'll get that paper into you by the end of the week."

Jameson walked the student to his door and left with her, locking his office. Fifteen minutes later he sat in his car outside the In and Out Mart, waiting for Tony to leave. He didn't want to talk to him at the store. Too public. He was sure he was following one of Scott's trails. He had an itch he always used to get when he was onto a big story.

When Tony emerged from the back of the store with a paper bag and drove away, Jameson kept behind him at a discreet distance. Will's brother took the highway to Savannah.

On the outskirts of the city Tony stopped at a laundry and went in, staying no more than two minutes. When he came out carrying only a sack, Jameson's curiosity spiked. A paper sack from a laundry? Next Tony visited another quick market, taking both sacks into the store. This time he exited empty-handed.

This was getting even more curious, Jameson thought. He followed Tony to a three-story, older apartment building, then let ten minutes pass before he walked into the lobby. If he had to, he would knock on every door until he found Tony. But thankfully he didn't. Mailboxes lined the wall next to the entrance. He spied Tony Blake's name on one and the apartment number was right below it.

Jameson found Tony's door and knocked on it. It swung open to reveal the young man, shoeless with his shirt unbuttoned and hanging loose. Tony's eyes grew round.

"Dr. King! What are you doing here?"

"I need to talk to you."

When Jameson pushed forward, Tony started to stand his ground, but after a few seconds stepped aside. The stench of stale beer accosted Jameson's nostrils as he moved farther into the living area. On the table in front of the couch lay a box of pepperoni pizza with two slices left.

"Why are you here?"

Jameson pivoted toward the young man with a day's growth of beard on his face and his hair pulled back in a leather strap. He had a wary look in his eyes.

"Tell me about the fight between Scott Winters and Kevin Reed that last month before you all graduated."

"Fight? I don't know what you're talking about." His brow creased into an even deeper frown.

Jameson covered the few paces between them and almost met the ex-basketball player eye to eye. What he lacked in height, he made up for by his no-nonsense expression. "Yes, you do. I know it happened at one of your little bashes you used to have."

Tony glared at him for a long moment, then something seemed to deflate in him. He shrugged and turned away. "There was always someone getting into a fight. Guys drink. Guys get carried away. How am I supposed to remember one from years ago?"

"Try."

With another lift of the shoulders Tony backed away. "Probably over some girl. That's usually what happened."

"I don't think so." Jameson moved forward. "I didn't drive all the way here to get the runaround."

"How did you find me? I haven't been living here long."

Jameson scanned the trashed apartment with some opened boxes along the wall. "What was the fight about?"

Tony stared at his cold pizza, then suddenly snapped his finger. "Oh, yeah. Ever since the accident at that last basketball game, Scott blamed Kevin for the end of his career. That wasn't any big secret. It was an accident, but Scott wouldn't listen to anyone. Stubborn fool."

"Why did he think it wasn't?"

"Who knows? Bitterness does funny things to a person." He looked again at his pizza. "Now, if you don't mind, I was in the middle of dinner and I would like to finish."

"Did Scott come see you recently?"

"No, I haven't seen him in years," Tony answered

quickly, but his gaze slid to the right and down. "We weren't really friends, so there was no reason for us to keep in touch."

Interesting, Jameson thought. *Like his brother, he's lying. Telling me way too much information when no would have sufficed.*

"Do you know where Kevin is?"

"I'm not his keeper." Tony walked to the door and opened it. "Goodbye."

Jameson passed him. "Oh, one more question. Where is Paige, your ex-sister-in-law?"

A tightening around Tony's mouth and a narrowing of his eyes highlighted his rising anger. He mumbled something under his breath, trying to push his door closed. Jameson stood in the middle of the entrance.

"Have I hit a sore spot with you?"

"She did a number on my brother. Spreading rumors. She did our family a favor by leaving. I have no idea where she is. Don't want to know."

Jameson stepped back. Tony slammed the door in his face.

NINE

Cassie knelt in the flower bed outside the newly renovated part of the Kessler Library at Magnolia College. The sun beat down on her, warming the cool air. A perfect day to start on the memorial garden. Along the brick wall she'd planned a row of azaleas with different perennials in front of them. She would use a few of the large bushes, planted ten years ago, that Steff had Trevor save when he'd begun digging the foundation for the annex to the library. Now that it was completed, Cassie could replant them.

After patting the dirt around one of the azaleas she moved to the next spot and pushed the shovel into the soft ground. Physical labor was just what she needed after all that had occurred in the past few weeks.

Again and again, she dug. This hole would be deeper for the largest saved bush, the focal point of the floral display. A film of sweat coated her forehead. Pausing, she mopped her hand across her temple, then struggled to lift the bush and place it in the earth. She should have waited for Jameson to put in this one. Panting from the exertion, she crouched and loosened some of the dirt around the ball to smooth into the ground.

Her hand grazed something hard. Looking down, she saw a dull oval piece of jewelry. Brushing the dirt away, she exposed a tarnished silver locket with its chain entwined around one of the roots. Carefully, she unwound the necklace and lifted it up to examine her find.

How in the world did this locket end up with the azalea bush?

Something was engraved on the front. She rubbed her thumb across the smooth surface. Initials? Possibly one a *P* or a *B?* Or an *R?* She opened the locket and a faded picture stared back at her, but she couldn't tell much from the photo. Squinting, she examined the photograph. Maybe a picture of a baby?

Closing the locket, she tried to clean it up some more with water from the hose and a rag. It had been in the ground a long time. She felt as though she had discovered someone's treasure. But whose? A student's?

There was something else. Some kind of date under the initials? Again she scrubbed at the oval piece of silver, but it was in such bad shape she could only make out the number 98—1998?

She nearly dropped the necklace when she realized the year was the same as when the woman had been murdered. The same year the azaleas had been planted near the scene. Maybe this locket was tied to the skeleton! No, it couldn't be, could it? Too much of a coincidence. But still, how did it become lost and end up buried so deeply?

The murdered woman had given birth. Is the photo a picture of that baby? Where is the child now? Of course, she wasn't even sure the photograph was of a baby. It could be her imagination working overtime, with all the intrigue she'd been involved in lately. Maybe, like Jameson, she should take up writing a mystery.

With trembling hands, she wrapped the necklace in the rag and stuffed it in her pocket. She surveyed the area, wondering if anyone had been watching her when she made the discovery. She wasn't even sure why, but with all that was going on, she couldn't be too careful. A group of students walked toward the library entrance, but other than them, the place appeared deserted. She shuddered. Fear permeated deeply through her.

She dug her cell out of her other pocket and called Jameson. He answered on the fifth ring.

"I found something in the ground when I was planting one of the bushes for the memorial garden. This azalea was saved when they started the renovation a few months ago." Again she made a slow circle, checking the terrain.

"What?"

"A necklace dating back I believe to 1998, the same year that woman was murdered. These azaleas I'm using were near where they dug up her skeleton. I think I should call Detective Anderson about this. Do you know his number?"

Jameson gave it to her. "I'm not too far from the college. I'll be there in ten minutes. I went to see Tony. I'll tell you about it when I get there."

After she hung up, she placed a call to the detective investigating the ten-year-old murder. He told her to wait for him at the library. She disconnected and looked around for something to do in the meantime. More students came up the sidewalk, and she gave them a smile, trying to appear as if she had a reason to be in the middle of a bed of dirt doing nothing at the moment. But standing out in the open made her feel as though she had a target painted on her back. She would be glad when the police arrived and took the locket.

Relief blanketed her when Jameson loped across the lawn toward her with Jim Anderson not far behind him. She sank down on a stone bench near the library entrance. Although she had dirt on her hands and the knees of her jeans, Jameson's look of appreciation as he approached wiped everything from her mind except him.

"We've both been busy, I see."

His crooked grin filled her with relief. "Jim's here. You can tell me about Tony after he leaves."

"Afraid he'll lecture us about doing our own investigation?"

"Yes." Cassie pasted a bright smile on her face and rose as the detective stopped a few feet away. "Thanks for coming." She stuck her hand into her pocket and slid the rag out of it, then gave it to Jim. "What do you think? Could it have belonged to the woman found buried?"

The detective carefully unwrapped the cloth and examined the piece of jewelry. He used the corner of the material to rub into the locket. "You're right. It looks like *1998* was engraved on it. Where did you find it?"

Cassie pointed toward the large azalea in the center of the barren bed. "The chain was tangled in one of its roots. From what I understand from Steff, that bush is one of the original ones planted ten years ago when they laid the sidewalk."

"I can't discount anything. I'll have the lab clean this up and see what they can come up with. It might be a clue. We don't have many. For the time being, please don't say anything to anyone about what you found. If it is a lead, I don't want the details to get out."

"Okay. All I could make out are initials, possibly a *P* and an *R* or a *B*, and *98*."

"They could be important."

"Of course, I won't say anything. I want to find out what happened as much as you do. I'm worried it could be someone I knew."

Jim regarded Jameson. "And you?"

"I agree with Cassie. I hope it's a lead you can use."

His friend studied him for several long seconds. "Keeping out of trouble?"

"I live a rather dull life."

The detective laughed. "Yeah, right. Why is it I get the feeling you two are up to something?"

"Beats me." Jameson stepped closer to Cassie, as though to present a united front.

"Have you had anymore hang-ups?" After putting the evidence in a plastic bag, Jim pocketed the locket.

"Not so far."

Jim started to walk away but turned back. "Don't do anything foolish, y'all."

When the detective was out of earshot, Cassie faced Jameson. "What happened with Tony?"

He recounted the interview with Scott's ex-teammate. "He was lying when I asked about where Paige was and if he'd seen Kevin. He knows more than he's telling."

"What was in the sacks?"

"I don't know. Something might be going on at the mart that neither Will nor Tony want anyone to know about."

"Enough to kill Scott over it?"

"Maybe. I want to find Paige. I'd feel a lot better knowing she is alive." He took her hands and brushed the dirt from them. "Are you finished for the day?"

All her senses were centered on his fingers wrapped around hers. Finally she realized he was waiting for her answer. Cassie peered at the garden bed she had prepared, trying to ignore the heady sensations his touch produced. "As soon as I cover that bush with earth and water the ones I planted, I'm calling it quits. Tomorrow I have a few high school students coming to help."

"And me."

"You still can?"

"I remember you promised I could drive the Mustang. I can't pass up that opportunity."

Men and their cars. She stifled a laugh and reluctantly pulled her hands away. "How about I pick you up on my way here?"

"Curb-to-curb service. I like that. What time?"

"Eight, and eat a big breakfast. We're working straight through until this is completed."

"What have I gotten myself into?"

"A day of fun with me and three teens."

At the edge of the new memorial garden, Cassie rose and brushed off her knees. She smiled at the distinguished older man approaching. "I told David I would give him a ride home, Dr. Rutherford."

The head of the English Department stopped near her. "I had to come see what would make my youngest son get up so early on a Saturday morning." He glanced over at the teens gathered at the other end of the flower bed. "Now I know. Who is he interested in? The brunette or the blonde?"

Jameson came up to them. "Christiana Ortiz, Edgar's sister. And they've just asked me if we could go to the Half Joe since we're through. At least, Christiana and

David did. Kathleen has practice. Her mother is coming to pick her up."

Cassie waved toward Kathleen, who was putting on her backpack. "Thanks. I appreciated your help today."

The teen began jogging toward a parked car. "Anytime, Ms. Winters."

David loped over to them. "Dad, what are you doing here?"

Cornell Rutherford laughed. "In case you've forgotten, I work here."

"Not usually on Saturday."

"Frankly, I was curious to find you gone when I came back from my jog this morning. Your mom told me you were volunteering for your counselor at school."

The tall lad's mouth pinched into a frown. "We're not through here." The frown disappeared the instant he saw Christiana walking toward them. "We still need to clean up. I'll catch a ride with Ms. Winters." He spun around and hurried toward the teenage girl.

"I'd planned on driving him home, so he's welcome to stay and go with us to the Half Joe. They've earned a treat."

"A coffee shop is a treat?" Disdain sounded in Cornell's deep voice.

"To a high school student, a college hangout is a treat." Jameson sidled closer to Cassie.

Cornell flipped his hand in the air. "That's fine. I have to meet with the president about the reception next week-end. I can certainly use the extra time."

"Great. You have a wonderful son. He's already showing promise on the high school basketball team."

Cornell peered at David helping Christiana put the last bit of mulch around the bushes at the far end of the garden. "Yes, he wants to be the next Michael Jordan. He wants to play for Magnolia College, then the NBA. That's *his* dream."

Cassie could tell it wasn't Cornell's dream for his son. In fact, from what little the teen had told her in her office, he didn't get along with his dad, which at his age of seventeen didn't really surprise her.

"Good day, Ms. Winters, Jameson."

As Cornell strolled toward the administration building, Jameson scratched his head. "I've worked with him for years and I still can't figure him out. He has three children and has always proclaimed what a family man he is. Yet I hardly ever see him with his family."

"David is the last one at home. Maybe he's trying to change his ways, become more involved."

"I could see Cornell doing something like that. He's campaigning hard to succeed Dr. Whitston as president after he retires in the spring. This little reception he was talking about is one that Cornell has arranged to honor our president for an award he received."

"I can tell you're looking forward to it."

His humorless chuckle peppered the air. "Like going to the dentist for a root canal." A gleam brightened his eyes. "But you could make it bearable if you'll agree to come with me. It's next Saturday night at seven o'clock at the Mossy Oak Inn."

Where she saw Jameson for the first time since returning to Magnolia Falls. How could she *not* go back there? "I'd love to. I'm assuming formal attire?"

"Yes, I get to dust off my tuxedo again. I have a feeling it's going to get some use this year with the race for the presidency up for grabs."

"You don't think Dr. Rutherford has it locked?"

"Maybe. It helps that he has a connection to the Kessler family."

"Ah, yes, his wife is related to them." She studied the slight tension around Jameson's mouth. "I'm getting the impression you aren't a huge fan of the good doctor."

"He plays the political game all right, and he's run the English Department okay, but I personally don't see him running the college." He removed his work gloves. "But I don't make the decision, so it's out of my hands."

Cassie glanced around him. "I see that while we were loafing David and Christiana managed to finish up. I don't know about you, but I've worked up quite an appetite. I'm going to see if I can talk them into going to Burt's Pizza instead of the Half Joe."

"I don't think you'll have too much trouble. Pizza and teens go hand in hand."

David leaned across the table at Burt's Pizza. "That's Marcus Reed coming in the door."

Christiana grabbed a slice of pepperoni. "David's day is now complete since he has seen the star basketball player."

David playfully elbowed the teenage girl in the side. "Hey, I think you're making fun of me. Dr. King, is he in one of your classes?"

"Not this semester."

"I can't wait till the season starts in a couple of weeks. Dad's got great seats right behind the bench." As Marcus walked by the table with his two friends, David lowered his voice, "They say he'll be going to the NBA after this year, that he won't finish his senior year."

Jameson caught Cassie's gaze. "That's what I hear."

"He's much better than his brother. He…" With eyes

wide, David clamped his mouth closed. He turned several shades of red. "I'm sorry, Ms. Winters. I didn't mean to bring up his brother. I mean with your brother…"

Cassie grinned. "That's okay. I'll tell you a little secret. I've even mentioned Kevin Reed's name lately."

Jameson noticed Marcus's two friends get up from their table and head for the counter to place their order. "Excuse me for a moment."

Jameson weaved his way through the crowded pizzeria, a few of his students calling out to him. When Marcus saw him approaching, he straightened his tall, lanky body.

"It's good to see you, Marcus. I hear this may be our year to go to the dance."

His mouth lifted in a cocky grin. "I predict we'll go to the Final Four."

Without waiting for an invitation, Jameson slipped into the chair next to the basketball player. "I need to get hold of your brother. Do you know where Kevin is?"

"No. The last time I heard from him was when he checked himself into a hospital to get clean." Marcus picked up the half-full saltshaker and tossed it back and forth. "He couldn't even make it through the treatment program. He was there a week and left. That's my big brother for you."

The disgust in Marcus's voice astounded Jameson. There was a time that he had worshiped Kevin. What changed that? His drug habit? Or something else?

Jameson withdrew his wallet from his pocket and slid his card toward Marcus. "If you hear from him, it's important that I talk with him. Please try to find out where he is. But don't say anything to him about me wanting to get in touch with him. He won't be thrilled if you tell me where he is, but I think his life may be in danger."

A tic twitched in the basketball player's jaw. "What kind of danger?"

Jameson scrutinized Marcus for a long moment, weighing the pros and cons of telling him what was going on. "The kind Scott got into."

Marcus palmed the card and stuffed it into his front jeans pocket. "Thanks."

Jameson could feel Marcus's gaze boring into him the whole way back to his table. Cassie's smile faltered, her eyes full of questions.

He gave her a slight shake of the head, then asked, "Are you all about ready to leave? I don't know about you, but I'm starting to stiffen up. All that bending and stooping."

Christiana glanced at her watch. "Yeah, I told Edgar I would be home by three. He's got something planned, but as usual he hasn't bothered to tell me what."

David patted Christiana's hand. "That's my dad. It's his way or the highway."

"How about that last piece of pizza? Anyone?" Cassie scooped up her purse and fished for her car keys.

David waited a couple of seconds, then grabbed the slice. "I wouldn't want it to go to waste."

While Christiana and David started for the entrance, Cassie clasped Jameson's arm and stopped him. "What did Marcus say?"

"He doesn't know where Kevin is," he whispered close to her ear.

"Why am I not surprised?"

He chuckled. His nearness even in a crowded restaurant caused a fluttering in her stomach. She moved back a little but kept her voice low. "Was he lying?"

"I don't think so. They don't seem to be as close as they once were." Jameson settled his hand at the small of her back and guided her toward the front. "I told him to call me if he hears from Kevin."

Cassie glanced over her shoulder. "I don't know if you should have." After they left the pizzeria, she made sure David and Christiana were out of earshot, then added, "He could be involved."

"We don't even know what's going on."

"Will and Tony could be running a drug ring. We don't know what was in those sacks Tony had. I could see Kevin in the thick of it all."

"But I don't see Marcus. His basketball career means too much to him. He comes from a poor family. It's his ticket out of that kind of life."

"We're no closer to what's happened to Scott than a week ago. I feel like we're spinning our wheels."

"I seem to remember you telling me I could drive the Mustang," Jameson said as they approached the two teens.

Cassie went around to the passenger's side and tossed him the keys over the roof of the vehicle. "I wondered when you were going to say something."

"This is a cool car, Ms. Winters." David climbed into the small back seat, sitting closer to Christiana than he really had to. "When did you get it?"

Cassie cleared her throat. "It was my brother's."

"I remember seeing him play basketball. He was good."

After Jameson put the convertible top down, Cassie twisted around to peer at David in the back seat. "You really do live and breathe the game." *Like Scott did once.*

"Yep. I wish someone like Marcus would practice with the team. Give us some pointers."

The wind played with Cassie's long hair as Jameson drove toward Christiana's. "That's not a bad idea. I've been thinking lately of starting a mentoring group at the high school. I'd match students with people in the community and at the college who are working in the field they are interested in as a career."

David's face split with a huge grin. "I'll volunteer to be the first one you pair up—hopefully with Marcus Reed."

"If we are putting in our preferences, I would love to be matched up with Dee Owens. I want to go into public relations," Christiana piped in as Jameson pulled up to her place near the college.

"I'll walk you to the door." Before Christiana could say anything, David leaped out of the Mustang without using the door.

Cassie noticed Edgar standing in the entrance, watching the pair walk toward him. Cassie waved, noting out loud, "He doesn't look too happy."

"His sister is beautiful and she is growing up. Boys are attracted to her. I imagine Edgar has his hands full."

"According to her, she won't start dating until she graduates from high school, if her brother has his way."

"A bit overprotective, I see."

Cassie indicated an inch with her thumb and forefinger. "Just a tad."

Jameson roared with laughter. "I don't envy him."

As a frowning David headed back to the car, Cassie climbed out to allow him to get into the back. "Everything okay?"

"Christiana invited me to church tomorrow, but I don't think her brother was pleased by the invitation."

"Are you going?"

"Yeah, and I'm sitting with Christiana." David's smile was slow and easy.

"This I've got to see," Cassie murmured.

Jameson threw her an amused look. "You go to the same church?"

She nodded.

Shortly, they dropped off David at his house, and then Jameson directed the Mustang toward his apartment building. All too soon he parked in front and shifted toward Cassie.

"I heard from Jim."

"Did they discover anything else?"

"He didn't come right out and say, but I believe they think it could be a clue to the woman's identity or to the murderer. Knowing crime labs, I'm sure they will be able to discern what the two initials are and the complete date."

"Which has got to be important. Maybe they'll be able to restore the photo, too. I think it was a baby picture, but I don't know for sure."

"If so, then the date could be a birth date of the baby. That could help the police possibly." He clasped the back edge of her seat, only inches from her arm. "Have you gotten anymore calls?"

"No, but there are times I feel I'm being watched. I never see anyone. I hope it's my overactive imagination."

"You're taking precautions?"

She wanted him to touch her. She wanted him to kiss her. "Yes, and so is Mom. And I see police cruisers drive by the house throughout the day."

"Good. Jim must have arranged that."

"Actually, I'm thinking those hang-ups were from a student."

He arched a brow. "Why?"

"I started making sure I answered all the calls, because the hang-ups always happened when Mom picked up. The next day I answered one, and it was David."

"David Rutherford, who just got out of this car?"

"I've been counseling him at school a lot lately. He and his dad are fighting. He needs someone to talk to. I didn't ask him if he'd been hanging up when I didn't answer. I didn't think about it at the time. But he can be shy and flusters easily."

"Do you think he'd tell you if he did do it?"

She stared out the windshield, trying to decide if the teen would. Jameson laid his hand on her shoulder, drawing her attention back to him. "Yes, if I explain the importance of knowing if he did."

"Then check with him. I'd feel a lot better knowing those calls came from a teen rather than the killer."

"So would I."

He started to remove his touch. She placed her hand over his, her gaze ensnared in the depths of his. "Come to church with me tomorrow. We can talk with David then."

He blinked, severing their visual connection. Dropping his arm, he faced forward, releasing a deep breath. "You don't play fair."

"You know the cliché, life's not fair."

He chuckled. "Okay. I'll meet you there. Where and when?"

"Ten-thirty at Magnolia Christian Church."

"I'd better go before you talk me into something else."

As he left and Cassie came around to the driver's side, she thought about her impulsive question. Surprisingly he had readily agreed. *Thank You, Lord.*

"I heard that Jameson talked with Marcus today at Burt's Pizza."

The killer's hand tightened about his cell. "Great. We can't let him find Kevin before we do. We'll need to keep an eye on Marcus, too."

"In the mean time I'll keep looking for Kevin. He's the root of all our problems."

TEN

"It's so good to see you again." Reverend Rogers shook Jameson's hand.

"Good sermon." The drill of Cassie's gaze bore into Jameson. He could imagine the questions tumbling through her mind at the moment. He wouldn't be able to escape without giving her some answers. Mentally he began to prepare himself for her inquiry.

"I'm glad you decided to pay us a visit." The reverend shifted his attention to Cassie. "How's your mother doing? She slipped out before I could catch her."

"She's helping with the refreshments after the service. She's doing okay most days."

"And you?"

"The same. I have to agree with Jameson. Your sermon spoke to my heart."

And mine, Jameson thought, and wished he hadn't. Until Cassie had reappeared in his life, he had been going along nicely, accepting what he had chosen as his path. Now he questioned his decision to walk away from the Lord. He'd seen how her faith had helped her through a difficult time—was still helping her. Had it been a mistake to turn his back on God? He'd been up a good part of last night wrestling with that dilemma.

Then he'd come to the service today, and Reverend Rogers had spoken about really listening to what the Lord wanted for us—not what we thought He wanted. In the middle of the sermon he'd sensed Liz sitting by him, telling him she was happy and content with the Lord in heaven. And she'd wanted him to be happy and content, too. He'd been so stunned that he hadn't heard the ending of what the reverend said. But he didn't have to, to realize that moment had been profound.

Cassie took his hand and pulled him forward. "I see Edgar, Christiana and David up ahead. We need to catch them. They don't usually stay for refreshments."

"Edgar, may I have a word with you?" she said out in the foyer near the double doors that led outside.

The tall Brazilian turned toward Cassie. "Yes?"

"I'd like to come see you about a mentoring program. I'd like to pair a high school student with someone in the field he or she is interested in career-wise." Cassie smiled at Christiana, then David, who looked as though he had swallowed a large dose of awful-tasting medicine.

"A college student with a high school one?"

"Maybe. For instance, David here would love to play basketball at college and, hopefully, professionally. Someone like Marcus would be a great mentor for him. He could discover what it might take for his dream to come true and what it's really like."

Edgar glanced at the teenage boy next to his sister. "Fine. Call my secretary and set up an appointment next week."

"It won't be just college students. I'm hoping people who work at Magnolia College will be willing to do some mentoring. Christiana is interested in the PR field. I immediately thought of Dee, who's been handling some PR for the school."

"You want to be in public relations. Since when?" Edgar couldn't mask his amazement as he stared at his sister.

Jameson felt pinpricks along the back of his neck. He turned slightly and caught Marcus across the foyer watching him, his gaze intense, his expression full of anxiety. Jameson started for him. Marcus ducked through the doorway that led to the classrooms.

"Cassie, I'll be right back," Jameson murmured, then hurried after the basketball player.

He wound his way through the long corridor crowded with parishioners, checking the rooms as he went. At the end of the hall he realized that Marcus had disappeared. Jameson stepped out the back door and scanned the parking lot. Marcus was known for his quickness on the court, which evidently carried over to life.

A hand on his shoulder startled Jameson. He whirled around and came face-to-face with Cassie.

She let her arm fall to her side. "Who were you looking for?"

"Marcus. I didn't see him in church."

"He usually comes in late. He left?"

"Yes."

"That's strange. He likes to stay afterward. I can see why he's so large. He eats his fair share of cookies." She stepped back so Jameson could enter the building.

"He seemed troubled about something. I was hoping to find out if it had anything to do with Kevin or Scott."

"I'm beginning to feel Kevin is the key to this whole puzzle."

"Yeah, I'm going to increase my efforts to find him."

"Anything I can do?"

He took her hand and held it up between them. "Take care of yourself. I don't know what I would do if something happened to you."

"Nothing's going to happen to me. I've got my very own bodyguard." She slipped her arm through his and began walking back toward the foyer.

He wished he was as sure as she was that everything would be all right. He had a bad feeling about this whole mess.

"You didn't tell me you knew Reverend Rogers."

"I wondered when you would get around to asking me about our prior association." He slowed their pace. "There was someone at the sanatorium he used to come visit. We kept running into each other. One thing led to another, and I began talking to him."

"So, he's tried to get you to see the error of your ways," Cassie said in a teasing voice.

"Well, not exactly. Mostly he listened to me at a time when I needed someone to."

Cassie came to a halt. "Have you ever thought that the Lord sent him to you when you needed someone like him the most?"

Shock held him immobile. Then the thought that Cassie had come into his life at a time when he needed her to show him the way. All of sudden he sensed the Lord surrounding him in a loving embrace, and the sensation awed him.

He needed to think. So much was changing in his life. He could hardly recognize the feelings swirling around inside of him.

"Cassie, I hope you don't mind, but I need to leave. I have so much work to do. I've neglected my novel. I—"

As if she knew what was going on in his mind, she pressed her fingers to his lips. "Call me after you finish your—work. Remember I'm here for you."

He retraced his steps and went out the back door. He couldn't handle seeing anyone at the moment. He was a loner. He'd spent most of his adult life figuring out his problems on his own. He just needed to be by himself, and everything would fall into place.

When he parked in the lot of his apartment complex, he couldn't even remember how he got there. How had his life gotten so complicated?

Cassie.

She was a complication he didn't need, and yet he couldn't stay away from her.

He slammed his car door as if that would rid him of his frustration. Two minutes later he faced an empty apartment and tons of work he really did need to get done on his latest novel.

But he couldn't move from the foyer. The urge to be around other people overwhelmed him for the first time in a long while. And not just anyone, but Cassie. He had only been apart from her for twenty minutes, and he wanted to see her again.

"I have it bad!" he muttered to the silent apartment.

A knock jerked him around to face the front door. Cassie? He hurried toward it and swung it open, only to find Marcus standing in the hallway outside his place. That troubled look Jameson had glimpsed earlier consumed his whole expression.

"I need to talk to you." Marcus pushed past him and walked into his living room.

"What can I do for you?"

Marcus inhaled a deep breath, then exhaled it slowly.

"I told Scott that Kevin was at that hospital. Not long after, Scott was murdered. I'm afraid I caused it, or something to do with my brother did." Words rushed from his mouth as if he had rehearsed what he was going to say and couldn't stop even to breathe.

"I won't lie to you and tell you Kevin had nothing to do with Scott's murder. He's caught up in the middle of this. I just don't know how. He might even be a victim, too."

"You think he's dead?"

"I guess it's possible. At the very least he's in hiding. He won't be able to hide forever, especially if he's still on drugs. He'll slip up."

Marcus raked his hand through his hair. "I know." He walked toward the door. "That's why if he calls I'll find out where he is and tell you. He will never admit he needs help. But he does."

"You've got my card. Call me day or night, the minute you hear from him. I'm worried about him."

Marcus yanked the door open. "So am I."

Cassie entered the upscale Italian restaurant and spied her group at the table in front of the large picture window overlooking Main Street. She scanned the other patrons at the Terra Cottage and saw a few familiar people.

Cassie made her way toward her friends. Jennifer smiled. Dee said something to her sister then nodded. Steff glanced at her watch while Kate took a sip of her water.

Cassie pulled out the last chair and sat. "Okay, I know I'm late, but the hairdresser was running behind."

"I like your new cut." Steff signaled for the waitress. "It's flattering."

Cassie touched her shorter hair, which still brushed the top of her shoulders, but now had more layers around her face and bangs that swept across her forehead. "It is different, but I was ready for a change."

"What prompted that?" Lauren closed her menu.

"Can't a girl want a change without having a reason?"

"It's a man. It's always a man," Dee said with a sprinkle of laughter. "I just haven't found one to give me a reason to cut my hair."

"It'll happen, sis."

"Yeah, this from someone who has found her one true love. How are the plans for your wedding progressing?" Dee looked toward the waitress, who stopped next to her.

"Great. We've almost got everything finalized."

Cassie gave the waitress her order last since she hadn't studied the menu. They rarely came to a restaurant so expensive for their get togethers, but because both Steff and Lauren were in love, they had decided to celebrate. She wished she could include herself in their group, but she didn't think that would happen after Jameson's declaration that he wasn't interested in a long-term relationship. And he was right. That was the only kind she wanted.

After the waitress left, Dee leaned into the table and lowered her voice. "I heard the police have a new clue. It's all hush-hush."

"If it's hush-hush, how do you know about it?" Kate took a sip of her iced tea.

"Because I have connections. It's a piece of jewelry with some kind of initials on it."

"I hope it leads them to the killer." Lauren's voice faded into silence. Her eyes widened as she looked at

Cassie. "Oh, I'm so sorry. I forgot about your brother. We shouldn't be talking about—"

Cassie held up her hand to stop her friend's apology. "I agree about catching the killer, but I also want to know who was buried under the sidewalk. When the police finally get an identity on the skeleton, I think things will start to fall into place."

"I wonder if the piece of jewelry belonged to the killer or the victim." Jennifer unfolded her napkin and smoothed it in her lap.

"Who's still missing?" Kate asked Lauren, who had run the Web site searching for any missing female classmates.

"In our class there are Payton Bell, Tamara Landi, Josie Skerritt and Paige Blake, I mean Tatum. Everyone has been accounted for. But then we have the other classes, not to mention anyone who worked at the college around ten years ago."

"I talked to Will about Paige. He says he doesn't know where she is, but there's something about him that makes me not believe him." Cassie wrapped her fingers around the ice water, relishing the coldness. The conversation was getting a little uncomfortable. As much as she wanted to solve the mystery of the skeleton, her energies were in finding who killed Scott, and why.

"I wouldn't believe anything he says. Half the things that come out of his mouth are lies." Jennifer shivered.

Steff stared at Cassie. "What I want to know is who's coming to tonight's reception? I hope I'm not the only one. Cornell has turned it into a huge production."

Dee frowned. "Everything is a big production for him. No doubt he's earning brownie points with the powers-that-be who decide the next president of the college. I'll be there tonight, making sure nothing happens that I'll have to smooth over in the press tomorrow."

"Seth and I are attending," Lauren said.

Jennifer stared down at her folded hands. "I won't be there."

"I'm coming to keep Dee in line." Kate smiled. "Brandon is sleeping over at a friend's. It will be fun getting out."

Steff turned to Cassie. "Did you get that new hairstyle because you're coming?"

Cassie nodded.

"With a certain college professor in the journalism department?"

Heat seared Cassie's cheeks. "Yes, Kate. Jameson and I are coming together."

"A date!" Dee clapped. "It's about time."

"I remember when she pined for him in college. She would leave his class all dreamy-eyed. He is a popular professor." Lauren peered into the center of the restaurant. "And speaking of professors, there's Cornell and the head basketball coach."

Cassie glanced over her shoulder and noticed Cornell with Zachary Kirkland. "Are they friends?"

"I don't think so, but Cornell is getting a tutoring program started for the basketball team. There was a good player last year who had to drop out because of grades." Steff waved at the pair, who saw her across the room.

"He's doing everything he can to cinch the presidency. Just as long as he makes my job easier. I'm worried admissions for next year will be down because of this bad publicity." Dee picked up the breadbasket, took a roll, then passed it to her sister.

"Well, the reception tonight will help put a positive

spin on the college." Steff gave the basket to Cassie without taking any.

She couldn't explain why, but Cassie suddenly felt a chilly sensation. She surveyed the restaurant but didn't see anyone looking at her. Even Cornell and the coach were in a deep conversation. She started to avert her gaze when she glimpsed another man joining the pair. Quinn Nelson sat, followed by a person she didn't know.

She's here with Jameson. The killer stood in the circle of guests and watched the couple enter the Event Hall at the Mossy Oak Inn for the reception for President Whitston. He tightened his hand around his glass so much that he realized it might break. He didn't need to call any attention to himself, so he forced himself to relax and regain his usual composure. He wouldn't let them ruin his life. They could be taken care of like Scott was.

But with them he would be prepared. Scott being home had caught him off guard. Never again. Too much depended on him remaining sharp.

"Would you bolt for the door if I told you I feel like Cinderella attending the ball with Prince Charming at her side?" With her arm brushing against Jameson's, Cassie paused on the top step and took in the glittering, elegant atmosphere from the decorations to what the guests were wearing.

"Don't you have that fairy tale mixed up? I thought Prince Charming met Cinderella at the ball."

She slanted her gaze toward Jameson. "A man admitting he knows the story, and he doesn't have any children. Interesting."

He smiled. "But I had an older sister who dragged me

to the movies and she has two daughters. I am a dutiful uncle. When I visit, I read to them."

"Oh, the things I find out about you at the oddest moments." She loved the little things she discovered about Jameson.

Amusement glinted in his blue eyes. "I think this will be a long night."

Catching sight of Will Blake across the room confirmed that for Cassie. "I don't like that man," she murmured.

"Who?" Jameson looked around them, his survey stopping at Will. "Ah, I think I know who you're talking about. I'll feel better when Paige is found."

"Me, too. She was pregnant our last semester. And the woman found under the sidewalk had been."

"The police are slowly narrowing the list of missing women down."

"Not fast enough for me. I keep feeling I knew the victim." Although the murder happened ten years ago, she couldn't shake the sense of having lost maybe two people in her life in a short period of time. How was she going to deal with Jameson moving on when her brother's murder was solved?

"Since this is a small-enough college, that's definitely a possibility. But for tonight, let's put everything behind us. Dr. Whitston deserves this celebration. He's been a good leader these past years. I'm going to hate seeing him leave at the end of the spring term."

Cassie started down the stairs into the Event Hall. "I think the fun has begun without us. Dr. Rutherford has outdone himself tonight."

"When you want to be the next president, you make an impression. Cornell has always been good at that."

"Ah, I see him over there basking in the current president's approval." Cassie gestured toward a group of people near the floor-to-ceiling windows along one wall. "There's his wife, who's Steff's cousin."

"He's no fool. When you're part of the Kessler family, you make sure everyone in the room knows it."

"I haven't seen Madeline Rutherford in years. She hasn't changed one bit."

"She has the money to take care of herself. I'm sure she doesn't spare any expense."

"And speaking of Steff, there she is with Trevor."

Cassie and Jameson joined the couple near one of the buffet tables, laden with a silver tray of crackers, as well as various kinds of cheese, vegetable and fruit platters, boiled shrimp and a glistening dish of caviar.

"I see you made your grand entrance fifteen minutes late," Steff said, moving off to the side after filling her plate with vegetables and fruits slathered in their special dips. "This is the second time today you've been late. That's so unusual for you, Cassie."

"I've decided it's fun to shake things up a little bit."

"What do you think of her new haircut?" Steff looked right at Jameson.

Cassie wanted to crawl under the table behind her now ex-friend.

Jameson made a production out of studying her hair, turning his back to Steff so she couldn't see him winking at Cassie. "New haircut? I don't see anything different."

The innocent look he gave Steff caused Cassie to brush her hand across her mouth to keep from laughing out loud.

"Men can be so blind...." Steff paused and stared into Jameson's eyes. "You noticed."

He nodded. "And as a dutiful date, when I picked her up I mentioned it as well as the attractive black cocktail dress she has on."

Trevor laughed. "Honey, I think this is a good time to remind you about checking the PA system."

"Yes, I promised Cornell I would do that for him. I'm actually surprised he delegated that job to me. He's been running around trying to do everything himself today." She started toward the front, then stopped and added, "I will admit it's been nice not having to do everything."

When her friend left, Cassie said, "It's good to see Steff so happy. I know you are the reason, Trevor."

As Cornell hurried past them to catch Steff, Trevor set his plate on a large tray nearby. "I empathize with Cornell. He married into the Kessler family, and I can tell you it isn't easy trying to fit in. Even though we're engaged, Steff's parents have never thought I was good enough for their daughter."

"You think Cornell went through the same thing?"

"I've seen him at a few family functions, and Madeline definitely has final say. That can't be easy for someone like Cornell."

Cassie searched for the head of the English Department at the front of the room with Steff. She'd never thought to feel sorry for the man, especially when hearing his youngest son talk about how heavy-handed his father was. Cornell, as Steff pointed out, wanted everything done a certain way and didn't tolerate mess-ups.

"Trevor, I was hoping to see you tonight." Zachary Kirkland joined them. "I've looked over your estimate, and my wife and I want to go ahead with the renovation project."

"We'll need to schedule a meeting."

"How about Monday at two before practice?"

Trevor thought a moment. "I can make that. Your office at the gym?"

"Yes." The head basketball coach shifted his attention to Jameson, then Cassie. "Cassie, I'm so sorry about Scott. I can't believe someone would want to kill him."

"Mom and I appreciated you and your staff coming to the funeral."

Quinn Nelson approached them and slipped in beside Zachary.

"Quinn and I were discussing doing something for Scott. I know you planted the memorial garden, but we wanted to do something connected to the team. I thought we would retire his number."

"Before his accident Scott lived for basketball. Retiring his number would be great." She could remember seeing a few jerseys framed and mounted on the wall in the lobby of the gym for all the patrons to see.

"Some of the players will be disappointed they don't get to wear that number," Quinn said. "Usually the honor is reserved for someone who goes to the NBA, but if Scott hadn't been hurt, he would have."

Thinking about her brother's missed chance produced a tightness in her throat. "I'm sure he would have. Several pro teams were actively courting him."

"Have the police gotten any leads?" the head coach asked, then stuck his hand into his pocket and withdrew his cell. "I'm sorry, I have to take this call. Excuse me."

While Zachary moved toward an exit, Quinn said, "He's expecting a call from a recruiter. We've all been hoping and praying the police discover who murdered Scott."

"So far they don't know much. If they do, they aren't

saying." Cassie's words came out in a raspy voice. She swallowed several times, but the lump of emotions lodged itself firmly in her throat.

Jameson slid his arm around her. "So the big question this year, are the Tigers going all the way to the championship?"

"The competition is stiff, but we haven't been this strong since Scott was on the team."

Cassie saw the men around her through a blurry veil. "Excuse me." She slipped from Jameson's loose hold and hurried toward the entrance.

She needed to escape before she cried in front of a roomful of people. She needed to get herself under control. She was halfway across the lobby when Jameson halted her with a hand on her arm.

"Cassie?"

"Let me go." She had to get to the restroom before she broke down in front of him. Tears swam in her eyes, and she averted her head.

He loosened his grip but moved into her line of vision. "Let's go for a walk."

Why now, Lord?

She cleared her throat. "I just want to be alone."

"Normally I'm a person who certainly understands about being alone, but Cassie, you aren't like me. Let me help you. I know that conversation was tough on you. It's okay to cry. It's okay—"

She lifted her teary eyes to his. "It's not okay." Her world was flying apart, as though for weeks she had held herself together but all of a sudden was dissolving.

He grabbed her hand and tugged her toward a door that led outside. When the cool night air hit her hot cheeks, it released the dam on her emotions, and tears spilled from her eyes. She mopped her free hand across her cheeks as Jameson pulled her down the path to a secluded part of the garden.

Tears are useless. Quit acting like a baby. Her gymnastics coach's words reverberated through her mind. At the age of nine she had learned to stop crying.

Now after years of suffering any anguish silently, she couldn't halt the flow of tears down her face. Jameson placed his forefinger under her chin and tilted it up until their gazes connected. He brushed the pads of his thumbs across her cheeks, then drew her against him, holding her close.

"Cassie, let it out. You lost your brother recently."

The tender appeal in his voice fueled her tears even more. "I don't—do—this." But as she declared that, an image of Scott in his coffin at the funeral focused her on the emotions she'd been trying to deny.

"Then maybe you should," he whispered against the top of her head.

She couldn't hold back anymore. Sadness and grief poured from her. She'd never see Scott again. She'd never tease him or come to his rescue. He was her baby brother—the little boy she'd helped raise because her mother had her hands full trying to make enough money for them to live on.

Chilled, Cassie burrowed into the safe cocoon of Jameson's embrace, seeking his warmth. She cried for her brother; she cried for all those times she'd kept it bottled up inside her. Finally when she had no feelings left, she sniffed and leaned back, wiping the wet tracks away.

"I think that was over twenty years' worth." Her smile quivered as she stared into his eyes, the lights from the inn just enough for her to see a lopsided grin curve his mouth.

"Do you feel better?" He cradled her face with such gentleness her aching heart began to hammer against her chest.

"Yes." She laid her hands on his shoulders, becoming lost in his look—a look that said she was the only one who mattered to him.

"Normally when I see a woman cry, I run the other way. But if it helped you, that's great."

"I had a coach who thought any tears were a sign of weakness. He would drum that into us until there was no way we would cry."

"It makes some of us uncomfortable because we don't know what to do."

She smoothed her hands across his shoulders. "You did just fine."

His grin broadened. "So holding you was the correct thing to do?"

"Absolutely." She didn't want to leave his embrace. In the middle of all this tragedy, she'd found love, but he'd made it clear he wasn't ready for any kind of commitment.

"Then I'm glad I could help."

She wanted to do the same for him. He might never know how much she loved him, but she could at least help him. "You know what worked for me can work for you."

His eyebrows shot up. "You want me to cry?"

"If you feel like it, that's fine. But what I meant is if you want to talk about your wife's death, I'm here for you. Keeping our feelings bottled up inside us doesn't solve anything. Something will give."

He looked toward a stone bench, illuminated by a

stream of light from the inn. He took her hand and led her to it, then sat. "I learned early to keep my feelings to myself. Then when I became an investigative reporter, that was constantly reinforced. I nearly destroyed my marriage."

He felt his cell vibrating. As the people around him continued to discuss the upcoming basketball season, he slipped away from the group in the Event Hall at the inn. He withdrew the phone and saw the number.

Clamping his jaws together, he rushed into the lobby and found a quiet alcove, then flipped his cell open.

"You shouldn't be calling me. I told you I would be at the reception tonight."

"Where's the money you owe me? I need it."

"Don't you mean the money you've blackmailed me for? Isn't it enough that I've been helping you out of your mess?" If he thought Scott's killer would murder his blackmailer, he would—no, that wasn't possible. He couldn't afford for something to go wrong. Too much at stake.

"No! You owe me! And you know why. I'd better get it tomorrow or—"

The unspoken threat bothered him. "I'll get it to you. The usual place."

"Yes."

The phone went dead. He snapped his closed and examined the area to make sure no one had overheard him. He'd let his temper get the better of him. He needed to watch that or he'd make a mistake.

ELEVEN

Sitting in the Mossy Inn's garden, Jameson settled his elbows on his thighs, rubbing his thumb across his palm. "I didn't want Liz to be involved in the ugly side of my job. Some of the stories I covered would have caused her to lose faith in humanity. She was such a gentle soul. I could never do that to her, so I kept quiet and protected her from that part of my life."

"You did what you thought was best." Cassie covered his clasped hands.

"Yeah." Bitterness leaked into his voice. "What was best would have been not being a reporter sticking his nose into places others didn't want me to."

"You were trying to make this world a better place. How did your wife get hurt?" She felt him stiffen beneath her palms, but she didn't remove her touch, nor was she going to let him not answer her question—not this time.

"As usual I was running late, and she went to our boat to prepare for our weekend trip. When she saw me coming, she started the engine, then hopped up onto the pier to greet me. As I waved to her, the boat exploded, sending her flying into the water." He shook his head as though trying to rid himself of images too horrific to visualize. "I ran to her as fast as I could, but by the time I dove into the water and found her, she'd been under for several minutes. She'd been hit by a piece of the boat and never regained consciousness."

"It was an accident. There wasn't anything you could do about it."

His gaze swerved to her. "The police discovered the boat had been rigged with a bomb. It was later linked to a story I was working on, but no one was arrested for it. Not enough evidence. Her killer is still out there." He hung his head. "The bomb was meant for me."

"Your presence there wouldn't have changed what happened to your wife."

He jerked up and twisted toward her. "She didn't want to leave for the weekend. She only came because I asked her to. We were having problems, and I wanted to try to work them out."

"What kind of problems?" For some reason she knew that was important.

"She was going to leave me. I talked her into giving me one last chance. I was determined to use the weekend trip as a time to open up to her. I thought if we got away from the city and my job I could. If I had let her leave like she wanted, she would be alive today."

"So you blame yourself, not the person who actually placed the bomb?"

He yanked his hands from her grasp. "Yes! I didn't want to admit our marriage was over. Her parents told her when she married me it wouldn't last and I didn't want them to be right. It was my pride that put her in harm's way."

"Is that why you left your profession?"

His piercing look sliced through her. "I finished the

story and it led to several arrests. All I can hope is that one of those men was the one who put the bomb on my boat." He shot to his feet and paced a few steps away. "But after that story, I didn't have the drive or heart to continue being a reporter."

"You became a teacher instead."

He prowled the small garden alcove, as though he could barely contain the energy zipping through him. "Purely by accident. I brought Liz home to Savannah and put her in a sanatorium. I felt the least I could do for her parents would be to have her close so they could visit her easily. I knew someone at the Savannah paper. He's the one who suggested I try my hand at teaching. He knew about the opening at Magnolia College. The rest is history."

Glimpsing the anguish in his expression, she rose and closed the short distance between them. "What aren't you telling me?"

His eyes grew round. "Isn't that enough?"

"If it's all of your story. I don't think it is."

"Maybe you should have been a reporter. You have good instincts."

"Which serve me well as a counselor. I need to be able to read people, because sometimes they don't want to tell me what is really wrong."

He inclined his head. "Touché. There isn't much more. For the first few years, I had hope that Liz would come out of her coma. I went to church. I prayed to the Lord to heal Liz. He didn't. For twelve years I went twice a week to watch my wife slowly wither away. And the whole time I had to face her parents and their anger that I was alive and their daughter was in a coma because of me. They never let me forget that."

"Because you let them keep reminding you. Did you think if you were miserable enough that would change what happened, that they would forgive you?"

Jameson sucked in a deep breath. "You don't pull any punches."

"I care about you." She so desperately wished she could declare her love, but she couldn't. "You've been punishing yourself and living in a self-made prison." She stepped closer. "Instead of turning away from God, turn toward Him. It isn't Liz's parents' forgiveness you need, but your own. The Lord can help you with that. Until you forgive yourself, you truly won't be living. Remember Jesus died on the cross for our sins. That includes what you think you've done to Liz and her parents."

He stared beyond her for a long moment, the quiet filled with an occasional voice coming from the inn. When he looked again into her eyes, something had changed in his expression. Or was it her imagination, trying to read more in the dim light?

He shifted closer, framing her face. "You are the first person I've shared that with. What is it about you that makes it seem so natural?"

My love for you, she wanted to whisper in the still of the night.

"I have to admit I haven't had many women friends to talk to. And guys don't usually go into all this emotional stuff."

I want to be more than your friend. She clamped her lips together to keep that inside.

His fingers delved into her hair. His lips hovered above hers. If she stood on her tiptoes, they would touch.

"I'm so glad we got reacquainted at the fund-raiser."

The whisper softness of his words brushed her skin. *Kiss me.*

The pull of Cassie called to Jameson. The fullness of her mouth drew him against his better judgment. They were friends. That was all it could ever be, and yet he wanted to kiss her. He shoved the urge away as he released her.

"I have learned one thing from all of this. I'm not good husband material." There, he had stated it out loud. His inability to open up even to Liz made that clear.

"You've come to that conclusion based on one experience?"

"I try to learn from my mistakes." He forced a lightness into his voice that he didn't feel. The emotional past half hour urged him to seek solitude before he spilled everything about himself to this woman before him.

"It's made you lonely, if you ask me."

He straightened. "There's nothing wrong with relying only on yourself for your happiness."

"Is that what you've been doing? Are you happy yet?"

The sting of her questions dented the armor around his emotions. "I don't know about you, but I'm ready to call it an evening."

"Sure."

He ignored the disappointment he heard in her voice and said, "Maybe we can get together sometime this week and go over what we have concerning Scott's murder."

"That's fine." She started for the path that led to the inn.

He clasped her arm and swung her around. "The truth is, I'm tired. I don't even know what to think anymore. Now you see why I'm not any good at relationships, even friendship."

Her eyes darkened. "You've made that very clear." She pulled away. "I'm tired, too. I think it's a good idea to leave."

He strode beside her through the inn to the parking lot out front. Her silence—one he didn't know how to break—taunted him the whole way to her house.

As he switched off his engine, she pushed her door open. "Thanks for this evening."

When he climbed from his car, she wheeled around a few feet across her lawn. "You don't need to walk me to the door. It's not like this was a date or anything." Then, without waiting for his reply, she continued her hurried path to the porch.

Sighing, he quickened his own pace and caught her before she unlocked her door. "I'm sorry if I've hurt you. I didn't mean to."

The glare of the porch light revealed the shimmer in her eyes. "I know. You've made your position clear all along."

He'd hurt her, and that was the last thing he wanted to do. *Lord, what do I do?*

A tear slipped down her face. The sight of it knocked the breath from him. He'd made her cry. Without thinking, he drew her to him, murmuring, "Please don't. I'm sorry, Cassie."

She cuddled against him for a few seconds before pushing back and swiping her fingers across her cheeks. "I guess I'm not through crying after all."

He tried to smile but couldn't.

"You deserve to know how I feel about you. I see now that a friendship between us won't be possible—"

Her words punched him in the gut. "Why not?"

"Because I want more from you than you are willing to give. Friendship isn't enough for me. I know that now."

Her declaration left him speechless. He groped for the right thing to say, but nothing came to mind.

"I can't tell you how much I appreciate your help this past month. Scott's death was hard on Mom and me."

That brought him out of his daze. "What about Scott's murder? Are you going to investigate it?"

She peered away.

"Cassie? Are you?"

"Did you want justice for your wife?"

"Yes, of course."

"I want it for Scott. I want to reveal to the whole world what he was working on that got him killed."

"You're not the police or, for that matter, an investigative reporter."

She turned toward her door with the key in the lock. "Good night, Jameson. I'll see you at our last class."

The finality in her voice wrenched him. Before she escaped into her house, he halted her and swung her back toward him. "You will not investigate on your own. Promise me, Cassie."

She remained silent.

"Cassie, I can't be responsible for your safety if you go off half—"

She pivoted away. "Hold it! First, you are not responsible for my safety. I am. Second, you can't tell me what to do—"

He yanked her to him and silenced her with a kiss. A kiss he had wanted all evening. His lips ground into hers for a few seconds as he held her stiff frame to him. Then suddenly she relaxed against him, her mouth softening beneath his. His arms went around her, holding her as close as possible to him. The fast beating of her heart matched his.

He didn't want to let her go. He didn't want this to end. But he had to.

When he finally parted, he said, "I'm sor—"

Her fingers stopped the flow of his words. "Don't tell me you are sorry for kissing me."

"I shouldn't have. It doesn't change anything."

Sadness invaded her eyes. "I know, and I promise you I won't do anything stupid. Will that satisfy you?"

"Yes." *No!* he shouted silently. He wasn't happy with the current situation, but he didn't know what to do about it. "If you discover anything, you'll let me know?"

She nodded. "Will you do the same?"

"Yes." He took a step back and held out his hand. "We are partners in this."

"Fine." She shook on it, then hurried into her house.

The door closing amplified how alone he was in the world—the way he liked it. Then why didn't he feel better?

That question plagued him on the drive to his apartment. He couldn't shake the dissatisfaction that gripped him. Even arriving home where he always felt a measure of comfort didn't alleviate the uneasiness. He had handled the situation with Cassie all wrong.

In his bedroom he went straight to his closet and found on the back shelf his family Bible. He'd put it away years ago. It was time to read the Lord's word again. Tonight he realized he wanted to be able to give Cassie more. But he needed to be whole to do that.

"Ms. Winters, I can't thank you enough for setting this up." David Rutherford held the gym door open for Cassie, who went inside first. "I still can't believe that Marcus Reed agreed to give me some pointers. This is really gonna help my game."

Cassie realized she didn't have to come along with the teen to meet his mentor, but she thought that maybe Marcus would be able to tell her something about his last meeting with her brother in the Half Joe's parking lot.

"Do you need a ride home afterward?"

"That would be great. Mom wanted me to get a ride with Dad, but I don't want to. He isn't too thrilled with me wanting to play basketball in college and professionally."

"Sure. From what I understand they are finishing their practice early."

David quickened his pace. "Maybe we can catch the end of it."

The enthusiasm pouring off David was catching. She laughed and trailed after the teen into the practice gym. Disappointedly, they came at the very end when the players were walking off the court. Marcus stood under the goal, shooting baskets. Zachary Kirkland said something to the young man, who gestured toward them as they came into the gym. After throwing them a speculative glance, his coach left.

Cassie found a place in the stands to watch while Marcus worked with David. From the wide grin on the teen's face, she was so glad that Edgar had set up this meeting. Just this week she'd counseled the boy because he and his father had fought again. Cornell seemed too busy running for the presidency of the college to see what his son needed—some quality time with his dad. Maybe when the position was filled, Cornell would do some activities with David, like shooting baskets. A giggle rose up in Cassie when she visualized Cornell playing basketball with David. She could picture the head of the English Department in his wingtips and three-piece suit standing under the basket, trying to make a shot.

Several players walked through the gym as they left, as did Quinn Nelson and Zachary. They said something to Marcus, then headed for the door. Cassie checked her watch and noted that a half hour had passed. She'd give David a little more time.

As she waited, thoughts of Jameson invaded her mind. She hadn't seen him or talked to him in several days. Tomorrow night would be her last class with him. Would it be the last time she saw him except by accident around town? When he had left Saturday night, he'd been wrestling with his past. She wanted to see his revelations that evening as a positive step in their relationship, but she was scared she was reading too much into it.

A movement on the court grabbed her attention. David gave Marcus a high five, and then the two began walking toward the stands. She came to her feet, seeing the apprehension in Marcus's eyes—as though he was afraid to talk to her.

She smiled, hoping to put the young man at ease. "Thank you so much for your time, especially with the season starting. I know how busy you'll be."

"No problem. I've arranged with David to work with him next week. He's got talent."

The teen beamed. "And I'm gonna sit on the bench at the opening game."

Cassie realized that Cornell, if he had been inclined to, could have gotten that for David. But according to David, his father had never offered. Besides, an invitation from the star player was a coup.

David shook Marcus's hand. "Thanks again. I'll be here next Wednesday. I'm gonna get some water out in the lobby. I'll wait for you out there, Ms. Winters."

As the teen trotted off, Cassie faced Marcus. "He'll be floating on air for days."

"I think the program you're starting at the school is great. I'm sure I can talk some other players into helping if you have a need." He started to leave.

"Marcus, I know you told Dr. King about telling my brother where Kevin was."

Marcus froze.

"Did he tell you anything about what he was working on? Why he wanted to see Kevin after all these years?"

Marcus hugged the basketball to his chest. "I wish I knew. When I asked Scott, he didn't answer. He assured me he only wanted to talk to Kevin to apologize, to tell my brother that he didn't blame him for the accident. That's the only reason I gave him the information. But…" The tall young man stared off into space.

"What?"

A long moment passed before Marcus said, "I don't know. He did something that made me think he was lying. He grinned when I said where Kevin was. When I called him on it, he yelled at me that I was imagining things. We didn't part on the best of terms."

That was the scene she had witnessed. "Thanks. I appreciate you telling me."

"I wish I hadn't said anything to your brother. Then maybe he would be alive and mine wouldn't be in hiding."

"If you hear from Kevin, please let me know."

Marcus avoided her gaze and turned away. Without responding.

She'd hit another brick wall. He wouldn't tell her if he heard from Kevin. She couldn't really blame him.

"Marcus," she called out before he disappeared into the locker room. When he stopped, she continued, "You didn't do anything wrong. Scott's murderer is responsible for my brother's death."

Again no response. Marcus's head dropped, and he kept going forward. So many people have been affected by what was going on. Her safe little world was being destroyed bit by bit.

She scanned the empty gym and shivered. Suddenly she realized she was alone in the cavernous room. Hurrying out into the lobby, she spied David by the vending machine, finishing a bottle of water.

Relieved to see the teen, she approached him as she dug for her keys in her purse. "Ready?"

"This has been the best day. Thanks, Ms. Winters. You're the greatest."

"Anytime." She strode toward the exit.

"Christiana told me she's going to shadow Dee Owens next week."

"That was an easy one for me to set up since Dee is a friend. I'll be interested to see if Christiana still wants to work in PR after spending some time with Dee."

"I'm glad her brother agreed. I still want to play basketball. Now more than ever." David climbed into Cassie's passenger's seat.

"So am I. How's it going with you and Christiana?" Cassie asked, pulling into the stream of traffic.

"I've seen her a couple of times, but her brother is always around. I've nicknamed him the Watchdog."

"Don't let him hear you say that."

David laughed. "I'd be out that door so fast my head would spin."

"You have to remember the Brazilian culture is different from ours."

"He's been here for years."

"Still, where we come from and our childhood has a big influence on the person we are." She thought of herself, then Jameson, and knew how true that was. "We're shaped by what has happened in the past."

Twenty-five minutes later, she parked in David's driveway. "If you need a ride next week, let me know."

"I shouldn't. I'll be able to drive again. Being grounded isn't fun. I hate asking people for rides."

"I remember the feeling. Next time, don't run that stop sign and get a ticket."

Sending her a grin, David hopped from the car. "That's what Mom said."

Cassie watched David until he disappeared inside his house before backing out of the driveway. Peering around at the large houses, sitting on half-acre lots, she hadn't really thought about what a nice area of Magnolia Falls Cornell and Madeline lived in. It wasn't Cornell's job that had bought the minimansion, but Madeline's family money. Being connected to the Kesslers would add a certain amount of prestige to the presidency if he got the job.

As she drove toward her house, she began to realize how far out of town the Rutherfords lived and how lonely the stretch of road between their luxury subdivision and the more populated parts of Magnolia Falls.

In the distance she saw a vehicle coming toward her. Behind her another car followed a couple of hundred yards back. Otherwise she was by herself on the two-lane highway. On her left she glimpsed some lights off the road that indicated a group of houses, but other than that, darkness blanketed the landscape. Not even the moon shone because of some cloud cover.

Her grip on the steering wheel strengthened until her hands ached. She forced herself to loosen her hold. Although the urge to press her foot down on the accelerator dominated her thoughts, she kept her speed under the limit.

The vehicle in the oncoming lane passed her, its taillights quickly vanishing around a bend. The car behind her sped forward, coming up right behind her. Its bright lights glowed so brilliantly that she couldn't even tell what kind of automobile it was. Not that she was very good at that, anyway.

Suddenly the car hit her bumper, jolting her. She pushed down on her accelerator. Her car surged forward, but so did the vehicle behind her. Her mind raced with possibilities, discarding one after another.

Sweat broke out on her forehead as the auto struck her again. Another spurt of speed shot her odometer above eighty on a winding stretch of road. In the lights she saw the curve up ahead and grasped her wheel even tighter.

Lord, help!

The automobile came at her a third time, but at the last moment swerved into the other lane and began to pass her. She chanced a look when it was alongside her, but she couldn't make out the driver through its tinted windows.

Then the sixty-degree curve loomed not ten yards away. A stream of perspiration rolled down her brow and into her eyes, stinging her. She blinked and kept her gaze trained on the tricky part of the road.

With another sharp jolt, she knew the mysterious driver

was trying to run her off the road. Desperately, she concentrated on navigating the sharp bend while increasing her speed.

The black car mirrored her move. Another thud. The sound of grinding metal thundered through her skull. At the beginning of the curve the driver collided with her left side and managed to nudge her car toward the steep shoulder.

Then everything happened fast. Her wheels hit the soft gravel, and she lost control of her car. She slammed on her brakes but continued her forward motion toward the dark field that ran along the highway. A grove of pine trees appeared out of the black curtain before her.

Heart pounding, she sent up a quick prayer and braced herself. The air bag deploying was the last conscious noise she heard as its impact drove the breath from her, slamming her against her seat.

Blackness, like the night, swallowed her.

TWELVE

Cassie heard a sound and wondered who moaned and why. As she opened her eyes, she tried to shift in her seat, but something held her trapped. Inky darkness surrounded her.

Where am I?

Then she remembered what had happened. Someone had run her off the highway. She pushed at the deflating air bag that had wedged against her. Leaning forward, she squinted, trying to see out the cracked windshield. What little she could make out looked hazy, as though fog had settled in around her car. She sniffed the air. Smoke?

What if the car caught on fire?

The question flew through her mind. Starting to panic, she fumbled in the seat next to her for her purse and found it, then searched for the handle and pushed on her door. It wouldn't budge. Her panic mushroomed into terror. Again she shoved on it, hitting her shoulder against the side panel. Finally, the door gave way and swung open. She tore at the straps of her seat belt, clawing them free, then scrambled out into the chilled night air.

The scent of smoke imbued the area. A gray vapor poured from the engine, the mist disappearing among the pine branches above.

Have to get out of here.

She half limped, half ran toward the road. Not five feet from the highway she glimpsed a set of bright lights coming from Magnolia Falls. She started to hurry forward to flag down the approaching car until she thought of the person who had caused her wreck.

What if he's returning to see his damage?

Fear drove her to the side, where she hid behind a large bush. The vehicle flew past, the driver obviously unaware of her smashed car thirty yards off the road. When it disappeared from view, she released the breath she had been holding and sank down onto the dirt shoulder.

Bruised and aching, she dropped her head into her palms. What should she do?

Call Jameson.

She dug into the depths of her purse for her cell and withdrew it. He answered on the third ring.

"I went off the Sheridan Road about five minutes from the Rutherfords' subdivision," she said without any preamble.

"Cassie? Are you hurt?"

The concern in his voice warmed her chilled body. She needed his arms around her and him whispering in her ear that everything would be all right. She needed him.

"Please come get me. I'll explain when you get here. Hurry." She clicked off before he started asking her a hundred questions, which would only slow him down.

She didn't want to be out here exposed for the maniac if he decided to come back and finish her off. Was he some drunk? Or was he connected to Scott's death? She didn't think this was a coincidence. The man driving had meant to run her off the road and possibly kill her. Why? Was she getting too close to the real killer?

If that were the case, she wished she knew what the murderer was afraid of because she didn't feel like she was close at all. She pulled her knees close to her chest and rested her head on them. The hammering against her temples intensified the longer she waited for Jameson to arrive.

Minutes ticked into twenty before she spotted another pair of headlights coming toward her. If he had hurried, that could be him. She had to take the chance it was Jameson. She shoved her body to a standing position and nearly fell when the dark world around her tilted and spun. Each inhalation caused her chest to ache. Cold burrowed into her, causing her teeth to chatter.

She moved out from behind the bush and waved her arms in the air. The car slowed down. Blinded by the headlights, she couldn't tell if it was Jameson's until it was a few feet away. Relieved, she collapsed against the hood, seeking the warmth of the metal.

The next thing she realized she was in Jameson's embrace, being supported by him. He guided her to the passenger side of his car and assisted her to sit, then knelt in front of her and cupped her face.

"What happened?" Tension filled the short question.

"Someone forced me off the road." She heard herself reply as though she were observing from a distance. The cold continued to seep deep into her bones. Trembling, she folded her arms across her chest.

Jameson shrugged out of his jacket and slung it over her shoulders, then rubbed his hands up and down her arms. "Do you know who?"

She shook her head. "Too dark."

Jameson glanced behind him toward where her car was. "Have you called the police?"

"No, I didn't have Jim's number with me."

"Why didn't you call 911?"

"This has got to be connected to Scott's murder. Jim should be notified." Her mind still in a fog, she rubbed her fingers across her forehead as though massaging it would will coherent thoughts.

"Are you hurt anywhere?"

Taking stock of her aches and pains, she said, "My head and neck hurt. My chest where the bag hit. That's all, I think."

"Here, let's get you completely inside the car and I'll take you to the emergency room, just to be sure." After helping her, he shut the door and walked around the front to the driver's side. He settled into his seat and started the engine, then switched on the heater and placed a call to Jim.

Still dazed, Cassie listened to Jameson answer the detective's question, but the words really didn't make much sense. She still couldn't believe she was alive.

Thank You, Lord.

Jameson flipped his cell close and then faced her. "Tell me what happened. Why were you out here alone?"

Somewhere in the back of her mind she knew she should bristle at his question, but she didn't have any energy left except to answer him straightforwardly. "I took David Rutherford home after he met with Marcus for a practice session at the gym. Marcus agreed to be David's mentor."

"Who did you see at the gym besides Marcus?"

She tried to recall the scene with David and Marcus. For a long moment all that occupied her mind was a blank screen. Then slowly images of people materialized. "I think the whole basketball team. The coaching staff. There were four, but the only names I know are Coach Kirkland and Quinn Nelson. Why? You think somehow I got too close to something to do with Scott's murder?"

"I don't know what to think other than someone isn't happy with you." He stared in the direction of her car. "For the time being, don't go anywhere alone, especially at night."

"But—"

"Listen, Cassie. You could have been killed or at the very least hurt a lot worse than you are. Don't give that person another chance. I'll go with you if it's somewhere you have to be. Promise me."

Her thoughts fixated on the words *you could have been killed,* and she didn't respond to him.

"Cassie, promise!"

The forceful urgency in his words struck her. "Fine. I won't. But how can you make that kind of commitment?"

"I'll find a way if it will keep you alive. I believe we're getting close or the killer wouldn't have tried what he did tonight. Now all we have to do is figure how why and who?"

"You had me so worried. Are you sure you're okay?" Cassie's mother hovered over her at the kitchen table.

"Yes, Mom. The Lord was looking out for me tonight."

Her mom sighed. "Thank You, God!"

When Cassie saw her mother's shoulders sagging, she said, "Go to bed. Jameson is here to keep me company." She gave the man who had come to her rescue and taken charge when she wasn't thinking straight a weak smile she couldn't keep in place.

"Honey, I don't mind staying up."

Cassie lifted her cup of herbal tea, a slight trembling in her hands still. "I'm going to drink this and then go to bed. I'm just too wired at the moment to sleep."

Her mother patted her arm, then left Cassie and Jameson alone in the kitchen. "I almost wish I hadn't called her from the hospital. It didn't take as long as I thought it would in the emergency room."

"She has good reason to be worried. And that isn't only my opinion, but Jim's, too." Jameson took a long swallow of his black coffee. "What that driver did was bold and desperate."

"Which could mean he will make a mistake."

"But at what cost?" Jameson frowned. "Jim wasn't too happy that we're continuing to dig into Scott's murder after all that's happened."

"He can't do much. It's out of his jurisdiction, and the Savannah police don't have any leads, at least not any that amount to anything."

"Well, at the moment neither do we."

Leaning against the table, Cassie rested her chin in her palm. "Maybe when my brain isn't so fried, we could go over what we've got so far."

"You need to go to bed."

"I would if I could. All I can think about is heading toward those trees." She shuddered and curled her hands around the warm ceramic mug.

"What are you going to do about a car?"

"I'll drive Scott's Mustang until I can get another one."

"Are you going to school tomorrow?"

Cassie glanced at the wall clock. "If I go to bed right now, which I can't, I'd only get a few hours' sleep, so I'll probably stay home at least until the afternoon."

"Good. I think you'll find you ache in places you don't right now." He finished the last dregs of his coffee. "Remember your promise to me. No going off on your own."

It had been years since she had answered to someone. It felt strange to now.

"Cassie! Are you reconsidering what you promised me at the wreck?" Tension held his body rigid.

"I should be irritated with you. What do you want me to do? Check in every hour?"

"I want you to take this situation seriously."

She kneaded her hand along the back of her neck where it hurt. "Oh, I take it seriously, and yes, I'll keep my promise."

He sagged back against his chair. "Then, when will you be through at school tomorrow?"

"After gymnastics practice. Around five."

"Good. Come by my office and pick me up. We'll go to dinner before the last night class."

She arched a brow. "Is this a date, Dr. King?"

"Well, no..." His words melted into the silence while his eyes grew round. "Actually yes, it is. I need to put my past behind me." He bent forward and captured her hand in his. "I care about you. I want to see where this will take us."

Her heart fluttered at his words. Her lousy day had turned into a good one. If she had the energy, she would jump for joy. Instead, she smiled and clasped his fingers. "When did you decide this?"

"I've been having a few conversation with God lately. Every evening I've been reading my Bible, and last night when I closed it I felt at peace." His mouth tilted in a lopsided grin. "Now, don't let this go to your head, but you were right. I shouldn't have given up on Him."

"I'll try not to." All the exhaustion she'd been battling for the past few hours pressed down on her. She slipped a hand from his grasp to stifle a yawn.

He rose and pulled her to her feet. "Come on. I think when your head hits the pillow you will go to sleep. Time to walk me to the door."

"You may be right."

He slung his arm over her shoulders and guided her from the kitchen. "I know I'm right. I'll see you tomorrow a little after five. I'll even let you pick the restaurant. Somewhere near campus so we won't be late for the last class."

She leaned into his strength as they walked toward the foyer. "I know what you're doing. You just want to drive the Mustang again."

"Am I that transparent?" He stopped at the door and faced her, smoothing her hair behind her ears.

His touch heightened her awareness of him. The rough pads of his fingers, his scent that reminded her of the ocean, the appreciative gleam in his eyes all centered her full attention on him. He dropped his head toward hers, slowly, as though giving her a chance to back away. There was no way she would. She wanted him to kiss her again and again.

The words *I love you* almost slipped out of her mouth, but she stopped short of them. She didn't want to add any more guilt to a guilt-ridden man. She knew the real reason he wanted to go to dinner tomorrow night. He was protecting her the best way he could, because of what had happened to Liz.

When his lips settled over hers, sensations whirled in the pit of her stomach. His arms enfolded her against him while he trailed tiny kisses to her earlobe.

"I don't want to leave," he whispered between nips.

Goose bumps rose from her head to the tips of her toes. "I don't want you to leave."

His mouth found hers again and laid claim to her. His hands delved into the thickness of her hair, holding her still. She felt as though a dream had been granted. Hope for the future took root in her heart.

Suddenly he set her at arms' length, his chest rising and falling rapidly. "I need to leave now. I'll see you tomorrow."

As he yanked the door open, she saw the war of emotions play across his features. Her hope blossomed. He wanted to be with her—not as a friend but as someone much more.

Jameson stood at the window looking out onto the campus. Not far away was the memorial garden he'd helped Cassie plant for Scott. Did everything lead back to the skeleton found months ago?

The ringing of his office phone jarred the silence. He snatched it up and sank into his chair when he heard Jim's voice.

"I thought I'd let you know that we found a black vehicle with white paint on its right side abandoned in a field not too far from where Cassie was forced off the road."

"Whose car?"

"An elderly woman who hasn't been driving for the past month because she broke her hip. Her car had been sitting in her driveway. She noticed it missing this morning and reported it."

Jameson changed the receiver to his other ear. "Does she have any connection to someone at the college?"

"Yes, she's the head basketball coach's mother."

"Interesting." So many questions flittered through Jameson's mind. *Is there a connection between the skeleton and the basketball team? What had Scott discovered? A murderer? And above all, what does Kevin have to do with it?*

"It could always be teenagers out for a joyride."

"Do you really believe that?"

"No. There were no fingerprints on the steering wheel. Obviously it was wiped clean, as well as the driver's door. That doesn't rule out teens joy-riding, but this doesn't feel like that."

Restless energy flooded Jameson. He rose and turned toward the window. "I'm not surprised. That would be too easy."

"I'm not going to waste my breath telling you to let me do my job. I've known you too long. Be careful." Jim hung up.

Jameson saw Cassie heading toward the English building. The strong wind whipped her hair across her face, and she kept trying to brush it out of her eyes. She glanced up toward his window. Her step slowed as their gazes connected. A smile touched her lips, which caused his heart to pound against his chest.

She had too much power over him. That scared him. What if she died like Liz? What if… He shook the depressing thoughts from his mind. Right now all he should think about was keeping her safe. After Scott's murderer was found, then he could figure out where their relationship should go. He couldn't afford to lose his focus on what was important: Cassie's safety.

A few minutes later a knock at his door alerted him to her presence. He crossed his office and stepped out into the corridor, ready to enjoy her company. "How was your day? Uneventful, I hope."

"I've matched a few more high schoolers with mentors, so I feel pretty good."

He guided her toward the exit, her scent of lilac teasing his senses. "I thought we could eat at the Mossy Inn."

"Sounds delicious. They have a to-die-for triple chocolate cake."

"I've had a couple of slices before."

"All at once?"

He chuckled. "Over a couple of dinners. I like chocolate, but I try to do things in moderation."

"I wish I could say that." Cassie tossed Jameson the keys as she made her way to the passenger side of the Mustang. "I've been known to have eaten two pieces before."

Shaking his head, Jameson tsked. "Restraint, Cassie. I'll have to show you how it's done."

"You've got yourself a challenge tonight at dinner."

Jameson drove the car out of the parking lot. "Dueling forks?"

"I'll have you know I wield a mean fork."

His glance cut to her face. "I like seeing you smile. You have a nice one."

Her cheeks reddened. "Thanks. I'll remember that. Although it's hard going around smiling all the time."

"Better than frowning."

Her laughter spiced the air. "True." She settled back in the seat, laying her head on the cushion. "I've been looking forward to this dinner and your last lecture all day. I need something to take my mind off what's been going on lately."

"So no talk of murder and mayhem tonight?"

"We probably should at some point, but frankly I'm at a loss. I don't know where to go next."

"Jim found the car that ran you off the road. It was abandoned in a field. It belongs to an elderly lady who hasn't been driving since she broke her hip. She reported it stolen."

"No one saw anything?"

"Not that Jim told me. Even though we're friends, he has no reason to share everything with me."

"Like the description of the locket I found. Nothing has been said about that. All they've released is that a piece of jewelry is a possible new lead in the ten-year-old cold case."

"There's still the possibility, it isn't." Jameson pulled into the parking lot at the inn. When he switched off the engine, he patted the dashboard. "I could fall in love with this baby."

"What is it about cars with you guys?" Cassie opened her door and climbed out. "You sound just like Scott. All his money went into this." She laid her hand on the roof. "I hadn't planned on driving it, but with mine totaled, I'm glad I have it."

Jameson caught her gaze. "And knowing Scott, he would be happy you could use it. He wouldn't want it sitting in a garage."

Cassie averted her face and started toward the entrance, hugging her coat to her as the wind slapped against her. Jameson rushed after her. He'd seen the sudden tears shining in her eyes. He knew from experience grief would hit her at odd moments. He could almost feel her hurt. He wished he could wipe it away.

He hurried around her to open the door to the lobby. Inside, the warmth chased away the chill of the approaching evening. "I'm glad we're in here and not out there. I wonder if a storm is blowing in."

"I haven't listened to a weather report."

Cassie was still turned away. Jameson stepped around to face her. "We don't have to go in right away. We are a bit early for dinner."

"You have your class tonight. I don't want to rush through our meal." She studied him for a moment. "Just one question. Are you going to be with me the whole time I'm not working?"

"Pretty much."

Her mouth scrunched into a frown. "You don't have to do that. I can take care of myself." She spread her arms wide. "I'm alive, thankfully, after last night because I can—"

He pressed his fingers against her lips. "Don't. I have to do this. Please humor me."

"Fine, but I'm not promising anything."

Her breath on his skin sent goose bumps up his arm. He let it drop to his side. "Thanks."

"It may be early, but I'm hungry, so let's eat."

"Even though it's not quite six?"

"We need to get back to the college by eight." She slipped out of her coat and slung it over her forearm.

But not before Jameson saw the large, dark bruise on it. Its sight mocked his ability to keep her safe. That was why he intended to stay close to her whether she agreed or not. When she was at school, he felt she was all right, but that left a lot of hours in the day that someone could get to her.

As they crossed the lobby toward the dining room, his cell phone rang. He fished it out of his pocket. "Sorry. I'll turn it off." He looked at the screen to see who was calling and immediately answered it. "Hello?"

"Dr. King, I know where Kevin is staying, and he has agreed to meet with you. He says he's tired of running."

THIRTEEN

"What does he mean by that, Marcus?" Jameson asked.

"Kevin wouldn't tell me. He said he would only talk to you. No police." The fear in Marcus's voice vibrated through his words.

"Fine, but I'll have Cassie with me."

"He wants her there. He feels she should hear what he has to say."

"Where do we meet?"

"You know the abandoned sugar mill near Riverton?"

Jameson pictured the run-down building he'd explored last year for research for his first book. Its collapsing facade and isolation had been perfect for a scene he wrote. "About thirty minutes out of town on Magnolia Road?"

"Yeah, that's the place. He'll be there in an hour. He'll wait for fifteen minutes, then leave."

"We'll be there." Jameson flipped his cell closed and slid it back into his pocket. "Marcus said Kevin wants to meet with us."

"When?"

"We have an hour to get to the old sugar mill."

"Why there?"

"It's out of the way. It sounds like Kevin has been in

hiding since Scott's death and doesn't want anyone to see him. I used the mill in my first book. It's got great atmosphere."

"But you write murder mysteries. I don't think that's a good recommendation."

"I hadn't thought of it that way."

"What if it's a setup?"

"That's always a possibility. Maybe you should stay back."

"No! I'm coming. I need to hear what Kevin has to say. He may be many things, but at one time he and Scott were best friends. I can't see Kevin being the one who killed Scott, but he may know who did." She grinned. "Besides, how can you protect me if I'm not with you?"

Jameson hesitated, wondering if it could be some kind of trap. Then he remembered the fear in Marcus's voice. He knew the young man's integrity and couldn't see him being part of a setup. "Then let's get moving. I want to be there first before Kevin arrives. We can check out the place and make sure there isn't anyone else there."

"We can even get back in time for your class this evening. You'll just have to feed me afterward."

"You've got yourself a date."

"I know where Kevin will be in an hour." Cradling his cell against his ear with his shoulder, he put the mike in his backseat.

"How?"

The deep voice hardened around that one word and renewed his fear of the man on the other end. "After last night's—"

"Failure to take care of a problem."

He frowned at the interruption and reminder of the

botched job. "I decided to listen in on Dr. King and Cassie's conversations. I thought I was in for a boring evening, but he received a call from Marcus Reed."

"Good. You know what has to be done. We're in this together. You need to do your part. No loose ends or we all could go to jail."

"I wish I had night-vision goggles." Cassie peered up at the sky, clouds racing across the three-quarter moon. "Hopefully the storm will hold off until we get out of here."

"We'll leave the Mustang where Kevin can see it. That way he'll know we are here. But I don't want to show ourselves until we know he is alone."

Cassie hefted her flashlight, one of two they had purchased on their way to the sugar mill. "At least we have these."

"Ready?"

After buttoning her coat, she released a long sigh and pushed opened the car door. Cold wind hit her warm cheeks. "We should have brought some gloves, too." She clutched the flashlight and switched it on.

Climbing from the vehicle, Cassie directed the beam ahead of her as she rounded the Mustang and faced the abandoned edifice. Its dark hulk loomed before them in menacing lines.

Jameson swung his flashlight in an arc across the stone-and-wooden structure. The east side lay crumbled in a heap while the west stood sentinel over the mill.

Cautiously Cassie trod toward it, picking her way through the gravel and uneven surface, marred with pockmarks, as though someone had dug small holes every few feet. "This isn't a safe place, especially at night."

"But it is very isolated." He nodded toward the terrain surrounding the sugar mill. "It's flat with few trees and hiding places. That's to our advantage."

Cassie surveyed the area and only noticed a small grove of trees silhouetted on the horizon maybe two hundred yards away. "I just wish my imagination wasn't working overtime."

As she neared the entrance, the wind sweeping through the building rattled the door. She half expected someone—or something—to thrust it open and explode outside. Her heartbeat matched the clattering portal.

"We aren't going in there, are we?" She pointed with her flashlight toward the steps that led into the mill, the beam wavering as her hands shook from the cold and a growing sense of apprehension.

"No, but there are several overgrown bushes off to the side that can conceal us."

The sweep of his arm directed her attention to the large plants several feet away, their branches flapping in the brisk wind. "Oh."

Jameson grabbed her hand and slipped between the stone structure and the bushes. Cassie followed, shuffling her feet to prevent tripping on the pitted ground. Safely settled behind the green wall, she knelt next to Jameson and switched off her light. Darkness closed in around her. He parted some foliage, and through the hole he created Cassie could see the outline of the Mustang in the dim moonlight.

"Now the wait begins. It shouldn't be long." Jameson's strong, soothing voice calmed the rapid beating of her heart.

"I'm surprised Kevin wasn't here waiting for us." She would be all right. They would discover what Scott was investigating and possibly even who his murderer was, and then her normal life could resume.

"He would have no way of knowing Marcus could get hold of me. And if he was hiding in Savannah, he has to come a little farther than we did."

"Not exactly how I imagined my evening when you invited me to dinner." Her stomach rumbling, Cassie leaned against the stones. "And I'd worked up quite an appetite with practice today. This will teach me not to skip lunch."

"Why did you skip lunch?"

"David was upset and needed to talk. Then after he left another student had a crisis. This seemed to be the day for problems." She shifted, trying to make herself more comfortable. "I did find out from David that he was the one who called my house and hung up several times. He apologized."

"That's a relief to know it wasn't something more sinister."

"I set up another practice session with Marcus for David."

"I image he doesn't get much attention from Cornell right now. He's been so busy staking his claim to the presidency."

"My mother had to be a single mom for most of my childhood, but she always had time for us. She sometimes worked two jobs to get enough money to support us, but she was there when we needed her." Her legs aching from squatting, she sat on the ground. "One of Scott's dreams was to go to the NBA and earn enough money so Mom wouldn't have to work anymore and could live a comfortable retirement."

"What were your dreams?"

"To teach, get married and have several children. How about you?"

"Put the bad guys in jail where they belonged." He settled next to her, his arm touching the length of hers. "That changed after Liz got hurt."

When he didn't continue, Cassie asked, "To what?"

"Actually, other than taking the best care of her, I didn't have a dream. I lived one day at a time for years."

"And now?"

"At this moment, I want to help you. I haven't thought beyond that."

"Hopefully this will be over soon, and we both can get on with our lives."

"I still feel I'm living in a limbo, but I've started reading my Bible again. It certainly has given me something to think about."

Two glowing beams, coming toward them, brightened the darkness. Cassie straightened, clutching her flashlight. A car stopped near the Mustang, and a minute later a tall man emerged from it.

"Dr. King? Cassie?"

She recognized Kevin's voice, although the person still was shrouded in shadows. She started to rise.

Jameson halted her. "Let me go first."

She nodded, even though he couldn't see her response. She waited while he pushed to his feet and slid along the stone facade.

"Give me a minute to make sure everything is okay before coming out." Jameson came from around the back of the bush. "I'm over here, Kevin. Are you alone?"

"Where's Cassie?" Kevin spun toward Jameson twenty feet from him.

"Are you alone?"

Marcus's brother went to his car and opened the driver's door as well as the back one. The interior light revealed an empty vehicle. "Satisfied? I'm alone. I'm not the one you need to be afraid of."

"Cassie, come on out." Jameson didn't move forward until she was at his side.

In the glow from the car, Cassie saw Jameson clasp his flashlight as if it were a club. She did likewise and almost laughed. She had never been in a fight before and had no idea what she'd do if she was involved in one.

Kevin kicked his doors shut and darkness fell around them again. In the faint rays from the moon she could make out his outline and the taut set to his stance. Jameson, with her next to him, halted a few feet from Kevin. Tension whirled around them like the wind.

"So why did you bring us all the way out here?" Jameson's voice knifed through the strained silence.

"Cassie, I wish for his sake Scott had never found me. He might still be alive if he hadn't been such a good reporter." Pain laced each word.

"But he did, and we need to know who murdered him. Do you know?" Cassie held her breath, her eyes slowly adjusting to the darkness.

"No."

Cassie blew out the trapped air in her lungs and stepped closer. "Then why are we here?"

"Because you have a right to know what Scott and I talked about. I think that is what got him killed."

"Why do you think that?" Jameson moved to Cassie.

"Because I've been hiding ever since I came back to this area. Someone tried to run me down about four months ago. I'm only a threat to one person. Coach Nelson."

The picture of the assistant basketball coach streaked across Cassie's mind. The short, balding man wasn't her idea of a cold-blooded killer. "Why would he want you dead?"

"He's the reason we lost the play-off game four years ago."

"How?" Skepticism was clear in Jameson's voice.

"He paid me to throw the game. I was too far in debt to say no. Near the end the only way I could see us losing the game was to take Scott out. He was hot that night. He would have won the game for us single-handedly. I didn't mean to permanently disable him."

"What kind of debt?" Cassie fumbled for Jameson's hand and gripped it.

"Gambling. Coach Nelson approached me about my gambling problem. He had a way for me to take care of what I owed my bookie. I never bet on basketball. I should have wondered how he knew about my gambling, but at the time I was too thankful for the chance to wipe my debt out to question it."

"What are you implying?" Jameson slipped his arm around Cassie and pulled her close.

"Coach Nelson fixes certain games and profits from it. I don't know who else is in with him or even if anyone is, but Scott came to me after he analyzed the past few seasons, starting with the one four years ago. He saw a trend. It wasn't blatant, but it was enough to make the coach a lot of money if he put enough down on a certain game."

Cassie quaked with anger. "How did he fix the games?"

"Probably like he did with me. He found someone vulnerable and offered him a deal he couldn't turn down.

I had to lose the play-off game, but a lot of the times a player only had to miss a couple of key shots to cut our win to cover the point spread. That would be harder to track."

Scott died because of a gambling scheme, because of someone's greed. The very thought appalled Cassie. "Then how did Scott find a trend?"

"He discovered something from Tony when he was investigating the women who were still missing from ten years ago. He had questioned Tony about Paige and Will. Tony has a habit of not holding his liquor well, and Scott could ferret out the truth better than most people."

"Is that all?"

Kevin shifted his attention to Jameson. "Isn't that enough?"

"Would you testify about Coach Nelson?"

"Yes. I want my life back. I've been running from my mistake for the past four years, trying to ease the pain with drugs. No more. I can't change what I did to Scott on the basketball court, but I can help bring Coach Nelson to justice." The tall man turned to Cassie. "I told Scott I wouldn't come forward, and he ended up dead. I owe your brother."

A little late, Cassie thought, tears blurring her vision. She needed to get out of here before she cried in front of both Kevin and Jameson. She shrugged away from Jameson and started for the Mustang.

Crack!

The loud noise swung her around in time to see Kevin slump to the ground.

"Down!" Jameson shouted.

Before she could move, another booming sound echoed through the quiet and something pierced her shoulder. Stunned, she looked down, and because of the dark, she couldn't see anything. But the smell of blood assaulted her nostrils. She touched her upper chest and felt a wetness.

"Down now!"

Jameson pulled her to the ground as pain radiated through her. Blackness that had nothing to do with the night danced before her eyes.

"Are you hit?"

Jameson's question reverberated through her mind. *I have to be strong.*

"Cassie?"

"Yes, my shoulder." She glanced toward Kevin, who was crawling toward the abandoned building, dragging his left leg behind him. "We need to hide."

"Can you crouch and move toward the mill? We need to get inside." Jameson positioned himself behind the Mustang, continuing to use it as a shield.

"Yes." Trying desperately to block the pain, Cassie squatted, using her good arm to keep her balance while her vision spun.

"Move as fast as you can. I don't want to be out in the open any longer than necessary." Jameson began creeping toward the building.

Progressing at a slower rate, her legs protesting, she kept peering behind her to see if she saw anyone rushing toward them. But the cars obstructed most of her view beyond the mill's yard.

"I don't see anyone. Do you?" Jameson asked as he neared the entrance.

"No."

"I think the shots came from the trees to the west. If he has a night-vision scope on his rifle, he'll still have trouble running toward us and aiming at the same time. At least I hope so."

Cassie visualized the killer hiding in the grove of pines, waiting for them with his sights directed at them. She looked toward their only shelter a few feet in front and noticed that Kevin had disappeared inside, the front door swinging in the wind, banging against the jamb. The noise rivaled her pulse thundering in her ears.

The gaping dark hole before them beckoned. Her shoulder throbbed. She could feel the blood dribbling from the wound, dampening her shirt and jacket.

When she came to a stop beside Jameson, she saw the elevation of the steps would most likely expose them to their assailant. "We'll have to make a run for it."

"We'll go together since the entrance is wide enough. He won't be able to shoot both of us at the same time. We should only be visible a few seconds."

An eternity if a rifle is pointed at you. But Cassie didn't see anything else they could do if they wanted to get inside. The two cars only blocked them so much. They had to find a better place to conceal themselves until help came.

Jameson grabbed her hand. "Ready? On the count of three. One. Two. Three."

Cassie surged forward toward the blackness, every nerve tingling with awareness as if she had a large bull's eye on her back. Which she did when she thought about it.

One second. Disregarding her wound, she dove through the doorway.

Two seconds. A shot rang out in the night stillness.

Cassie tensed. The ache in her shoulder intensified.

The bullet struck the building near Cassie's ear. The

sound exploded in her head. Wood splintered in a hundred different directions, slithers stabbing her cheek.

Three seconds. A dark cloak swallowed her within its folds. Jameson shielded her with his body as he shoved her toward the side, out of view.

Four seconds. Safe for the time being, but the pain in her cheek and shoulder threatened to steal her breath. She forced herself to take as deep an inhalation as possible. She couldn't pass out now.

Jameson punched in some numbers on his cell. Although Cassie heard his call for help, the pounding in her head struck the sides of her skull as though a drum were beating inside her.

Before she realized that he had pocketed his phone, Jameson clasped her arm and began dragging her forward. "I think I see where we can hide until the police get here. This place hasn't changed much since last year."

For a moment her legs refused to function. Her body shook with fatigue as more blood oozed out of her wound. A sound by the cars prodded her into action.

Lord, help.

Jameson stumbled into something, the noise paralyzing Cassie. The killer had to have heard.

Jameson didn't break stride. He pulled her, and she hurried after him, her leg brushing against what Jameson had obviously run into.

Passing into another room at the back, Cassie glanced toward the entrance and saw a dark outline of a tall man in the doorway. Quaking, she hastened her step inside before he spied her.

"Put your hand on my back. Follow where I go," Jameson whispered against her ear, so softly he wasn't even sure she heard until she nodded.

Jameson slowed his pace as he felt his way around the perimeter, one arm out in front in case he encountered another obstruction in their path. If his memory served him, there were a series of low cabinets in an office along the back wall where Cassie could squeeze inside. Then he would try to take care of their pursuer, or at least draw him away from her. He had to protect her at all costs.

He touched the edge of the cabinets, patted his hand along the wooden surface until he found a knob to open one. Then he leaned close to her.

"Get inside and don't come out until I tell you."

She hesitated as though she wanted to say something.

"Now," he whispered against her ear, then pushed her down.

She wedged herself into the small cramped cabinet, and he closed the door.

Momentary relief chilled the sweat on his brow. Then noises from the outer room, as though their pursuer didn't care that they heard him, made Jameson realize the man had nothing to lose.

Taking the same route back to the office entrance, he hurried his pace. The police were at least fifteen or twenty minutes away. A long time when a man possibly wearing night vision goggles was hunting them with a rifle.

His eyes accustomed to the dark, Jameson peered around the doorjamb into the large outer area. Moon rays streamed through a hole in the roof and dabbled across strewn boards from a wall collapsing.

A tall figure, shrouded in blackness, stood before a gap in the wooden panel. He lifted his rifle and pointed it toward the hole.

"Come out. You can't escape me."

That voice. He'd heard it before. He'd met their pursuer—recently!

"I know you're in there. I see your blood." The man knelt before the dark chasm, rifle poised and ready to fire.

Jameson crept forward, praying he didn't make any noise as he moved toward the killer.

"You're making me mad," the raspy voice taunted.

A shot went off in the stillness. Jameson jerked back.

Squashed into the tiny space, Cassie flinched at the sound of a gunshot. Tears instantly sprang into her eyes.

Jameson! No!

Lord, please don't let it be Jameson. Please. Please. I beg You.

She started to shove on the cabinet door, ignoring the pain impaling her with each movement. She had to help him.

"If that didn't find its mark, I'm sure my next one will," the killer cackled.

More prepared for the blast of the rifle this time, Jameson kept creeping toward their assailant when the second shot went off. Although it seemed forever, no more than a few minutes had passed. If he could reach the killer, he might be able to tackle him, and if Kevin was in the hole, save the young man.

"Okay. Okay. I'm coming out." Pain drenched Kevin's voice.

A minute crawled by, and still Kevin hadn't appeared in the opening of the hole, illuminated in moonlight. The tall man inched closer to the wall and jammed the rifle into the darkness. A shot echoed through the space where the young ballplayer hid.

A groan sent chills down Jameson's spine. He couldn't wait any longer. He'd have to risk rushing the killer even though several yards separated them.

Their pursuer bent farther toward the gap, his head inside the hole. Jameson made his move, sprinting forward. In his haste he knocked over something in the darkness, its sound echoing through the room.

Only three feet away, the tall man yanked away from the crevice and sprang to his feet with the rifle grasped in his hands. In the faint moonlight silhouetting the killer, Jameson saw night-vision goggles covering nearly half of the pursuer's face.

Two feet.

The man locked on Jameson immediately in the blackness and raised his weapon. Jameson swiveled to the side and went in low. The explosion of the rifle shattered the quiet.

Cassie struggled to her feet, gripping the edge of the cabinet to keep herself upright. With her wet, sticky shirt plastered against her shoulder and left side, she tried to get her bearings in the ebony curtain before her.

I can do this.

She bolstered her flagging energy with thoughts of helping Jameson. Another shot echoed through the air, followed by a groan. Jameson! Its sound demolished what strength she had mustered. She faltered and nearly collapsed to the floor. Catching herself with both hands on the end of the cabinets, she clamped her scream of pain inside her throat.

Her mind swam with dizzying circles of darkness. She swayed. Her right hand tightened around the edge of the wood as she sucked in swallows of air. She heard someone say something, but the pounding in her head intensified to a roar, blocking all sound but the rapid beat of her heart.

A few seconds later that roar was pierced by another blast.

She gritted her teeth and pushed herself away from the cabinet, running her right hand along the wall, as Jameson had done earlier, to make her way toward the doorway. She would go down fighting, not cowering in the corner.

Focused on saving Jameson, she stepped into the outer room. Grunts and scuffling noises came from the far side along the part of the wall that had collapsed partially. Was Jameson fighting with the killer?

Cassie crouched and felt for some kind of weapon she could use. Although she had a flashlight, it wasn't big enough to do much damage. Her hand grabbed hold of a slab of wood. She rose with it in her grasp and hurried toward the sounds. Nearer, she saw two bodies rolling on the floor; occasionally a shaft of moonlight revealed the pair. When Jameson ended up on the bottom, the tall man straddling him, alarm propelled Cassie faster.

The killer hammered his fist into Jameson's face. "Old man, you're a dead—"

Cassie swung her club and struck the man on the side of the head. The killer stiffened, then slumped forward, covering Jameson.

Cassie scrambled toward him. "Jameson, are you okay?"

He shoved their assailant from him and sat up. In the moonlight Cassie felt, more than she actually saw, the glare directed at her, her jolt of adrenaline exhausted. She sank to the floor.

"You were supposed to stay hidden."

She heard the words, but they seemed so far way. She opened her mouth to say something, but the dark void consumed her.

FOURTEEN

Jameson caught Cassie as she crumpled. In the distance sirens announced the arrival of the police within the next few minutes.

With a trembling hand he felt for her pulse at the side of her neck. *Please, Lord, don't let anything happen to her.* He prayed the same thing over and over as he located her beating pulse.

He cradled her against him, not caring that her blood soaked him. "You will not die on me. Do you hear?" His panic-laden voice came out in a rasp as he smoothed her hair from her face, willing his strength into her. Why hadn't she stayed where he'd told her?

She could have been shot again. She could still die.

He knew she'd lost a lot of blood. His panic and worry mushroomed while the screech of cars coming to a halt meant the cavalry had arrived.

Possibly too late for Cassie and Kevin.

Light poured into the abandoned building as the police streamed in.

Jameson blinked at the sudden brightness that assaulted his eyes. He shielded his face and said, "I'm over here. There are several people hurt."

More sirens filled the night. Chaos suddenly descended on the mill.

One man came forward quickly. "Jameson?"

"Jim?" Jameson sagged, embracing Cassie against him.

"Yeah, it's me. I thought I told you to stay out of trouble."

"I guess I'm not the only one who doesn't listen to directions."

Jim stepped over to the sprawled figure on the floor a few feet away and shone his light in the man's face. The detective bent down and removed the goggles.

"You know, this shouldn't surprise me one bit."

Jameson twisted around to get a better look at their assailant.

Cassie didn't want to open her eyes. Her lids weighed a ton. She shifted on the softness beneath her, causing her sore body to scream in protest. The dark peacefulness called to her, and she felt herself sinking back into the black void.

"She's waking up."

The sound of her mother's voice, full of distress, lured her back. She didn't want her mom to worry anymore. But she ached everywhere. She wanted to surrender again, but warm fingers grasped her hand and pulled her the rest of the way to alertness.

She batted her eyelids, the bright daylight assaulting her. "Mom." Was that her voice that cracked?

"Honey, I'm right here. So is Jameson. We've been so worried about you. You're safe now, at the hospital."

Her mouth parched, Cassie tried to swallow to moisten her throat, but she had no saliva. This time when she opened her eyes she inched them up to a mere slit. "Wa-ter."

Jameson came into view with a plastic mauve cup in his grasp. His face, lined with fatigue, sent relief through her. He was all right. His hand quivered as he brought the drink to her lips. For a second her gaze honed in on his wedding ring that he still wore. She looked away, not having the strength to deal with the hopelessness its sight generated in her.

The cool liquid slid down her throat, momentarily satisfying her thirst. She tried to smile, but it hurt, so instead she murmured, "Thanks."

He didn't say anything, but stood back and let her mother move in again.

"You gave me a terrible fright, Cassie. I thought I'd lost you like Sc..." Tears shimmered in her mother's eyes and rolled down her cheeks. "I don't know what I would do if I lost you and Scott."

"I'm fine, Mom." She hoped she sounded reassuring, because she certainly didn't feel it.

"Well, my dear, you don't look fine."

A dull, throbbing pain spread out from her shoulder. For a few seconds she couldn't remember why she hurt. Then she remembered what had happened at the sugar mill. She peered around her mother at Jameson, who stood hovering by the door.

"Kevin?"

"He's still in surgery, but the doctors think he'll make it. I should go check on him." His face was unreadable.

Her mother glanced from her to Jameson. "Here, let me find out how the surgery is going."

Before Jameson could stop her, her mother strode past him and out the door, leaving him and Cassie alone. He stared at her for a long, strained moment. He could still remember holding Victoria while Cassie had been in surgery to repair her shoulder. He'd felt so helpless, and emotions he'd experienced with Liz came crashing down on him all over again.

When he loved, he loved too deeply. He couldn't go through another loss like Liz. For twelve years, his life had been on hold. Lately he'd just begun to live again.

"Who did this?" she finally asked.

He didn't come near the bed but stayed by the door, poised and ready to take flight. "Will Blake was the one who attacked us."

"That doesn't surprise me. But what's he got to do with Scott's death?"

"According to Jim, Will has a very good alibi for Scott's murder. He was in Chicago at the time, so I'm not sure he has anything to do with your brother's murder."

"Then why was he after us?"

He laughed, but he felt no humor in the situation. "It's funny how quick you want to cut a deal when you're caught in the act. Three counts of attempted murder carry a long sentence."

"What kind of deal?" Her forehead furrowed, Cassie adjusted the bed so she sat up more.

He wanted so desperately to walk to her and smooth away the lines. He clenched his hands at his sides and didn't move. Glancing down, he caught sight of his wedding band, and all it symbolized to him overwhelmed him for a moment.

"Jameson?"

"It seems Will is involved in a point-shaving scheme with the assistant basketball coach, Quinn Nelson. They were partners. Jim is bringing the coach in as we speak."

She massaged her temple. "Was that what was going on in the back room at the mart?"

"Maybe. Jim sent some uniformed officers to raid the place before they cleared everything out. I have a feeling this has far-reaching effects. Will does more than point-shaving. He's a bookie for all kinds of illegal gambling."

"More people involved?"

"Probably. At the very least, Will's brother is running numbers to places in Savannah. The police there are picking him up. I have a feeling he'll talk, too."

"But who killed Scott if Will didn't? His brother? Coach Nelson?"

"Possibly. Or someone else?"

She frowned. "Who?"

"I don't know. I do know Quinn isn't that smart to keep something like this quiet. This point-shaving has been going on for at least five years. According to Will, since your brother's junior year."

"But that year the Tigers won almost all of their games."

"You don't have to lose to make money on the team. That's the beauty of point-shaving."

"No wonder Scott was determined to get to the bottom of it. He lost his chance at an NBA career because of them." Cassie fumbled for the cup of water on the table next to her and took a deep drink.

"We'll know more after Jim questions Quinn. It'll be interesting to see if he has an alibi for Scott's murder. He's the one I think had the most to lose."

"Scott thought highly of the coaching staff at the college. If he knew about Coach Nelson, this would have devastated him."

"I think he knew. That's probably why he wanted to

talk to us. When the truth comes out, this will open a wider investigation of the team. Everyone will be scrutinized. It could lead to sanctions against the program."

Cassie rubbed her hand across her forehead. "Poor Scott."

"We'll probably never know how he stumbled across the point-shaving scheme, but I think it had to do with his visit to the mart to talk to Will about Paige. I think he saw something that made him dig for some answers. Then when he talked with Kevin and Tony, he put two and two together."

"So his investigation into the identity of the skeleton is what started this."

"And I don't think this is the end of it. The police still haven't identified the woman."

"I wish we could find Scott's notebook. There might be something in it to help the police." Cassie stifled a yawn, but her eyelids drifted closed for a few seconds.

The yearning to hold Cassie overwhelmed Jameson. He stepped back against the door. She was tired and so was he. This wasn't the time to tell her they shouldn't even be friends. He couldn't be Cassie's friend and not want more. And wanting more left him too vulnerable.

"I'd better go so you can get some rest." He grasped the door handle.

"Jameson, please don't leave. We need to talk." Cassie closed her eyes again, but they immediately popped back open.

"There isn't anything we need to discuss. You're safe now." He yanked the door toward him. "I'll see you..." He fled out into the hospital corridor, not wanting to lie to her.

He didn't know how he could see her and not want to

be with her, and yet the panic, guilt and distress he'd experienced at the sugar mill and later in the waiting room plunged him back to a place he never wanted to live in again.

Lord, what do I do?

He quickened his pace toward the exit. He'd been in the hospital too long. He needed fresh air. He hated the smells associated with this place. He'd smelled them each time he'd visited Liz. For twelve long years they had been a part of his life.

Outside he inhaled the crisp November air. He couldn't seem to get enough. His lungs craved the light scent of pine. Slowly, the antiseptic odor faded from his mind.

He headed for his car, which Jim had delivered to the hospital for him. Behind the wheel, Jameson gripped the steering wheel but didn't put the key into the ignition. Staring out the windshield, he saw nothing of the parking lot. His thoughts reeled with images from the night before. Totally exhausted, he couldn't rid his mind of them. He relived the fear and guilt all over again.

Feeling Cassie's sticky blood. Smelling it. Pushing her into a space too small for her, knowing the cramped area would put pressure on her wound. Cause her more pain. The pure terror when he'd glimpsed her right before she swung the board.

Heart hammering, Jameson rested his head on the cold plastic of his steering wheel. What he would give to surrender to sleep right here in the parking lot. He needed to drive—

A rapping sound on his window drew his attention. Reverend Rogers stood by Jameson's car with concern in his gaze. Jameson couldn't even lift his hand to open the door. Cassie's minister did.

Reverend Rogers leaned down. "You look exhausted. You shouldn't be driving. Let me take you home."

"That's okay. I can—"

"I insist. My car is right over there." The man pointed to the next row.

Jameson didn't have the energy to argue. The past eighteen hours had finally caught up with him, and if he was truthful with himself, he knew he shouldn't drive, either.

A minute later he ensconced himself in the passenger side of the minister's car, leaning his head against the cushion. "I appreciate this."

"I was coming up to see Cassie when I saw you. I thought she'd come out of the surgery and would be fine."

"She is."

Reverend Rogers sighed. "Good. You looked so upset I was sure something had gone wrong with Cassie after the surgery." Starting his car, he glanced at Jameson. "So what is wrong?"

Everything. When the reverend let the silence lengthen, Jameson finally admitted part of the problem. "Cassie could have been killed last night. She took an unnecessary risk that could have led to her death."

"I keep hearing the word *could.* It didn't happen. Cassie is going to be okay. Life is full of all kinds of possibilities, but we shouldn't dwell on the what-ifs." The pastor pulled out into traffic. "Where do you live?"

After Jameson told him the address, he said what was really bothering him. "I keep surviving while the people I love get hurt, die."

"And you feel guilty about it?"

Jameson nodded, then realized the reverend's attention was on the car in front of them. "Yes."

"What would have happened to Cassie if you hadn't been there with her last night?"

Jameson pictured in his mind Will stalking her through the abandoned building and finishing the job. He shuddered. "She might have been killed."

"God is awesome. He gave you and Cassie just what you needed when you needed it."

Jameson closed his eyes. He hadn't considered it that way. What if he hadn't teamed up with Cassie and she had investigated Scott's death on her own? Would she be dead right now? He didn't have an answer to those questions. They weighed him down with even more exhaustion. All he wanted to do right now was sleep….

Someone shook Jameson awake. He bolted upright and noticed his apartment building looming before him. He peered at Reverend Rogers. "Thanks for bringing me home."

"Get some rest. If you need to talk some more later, you know where to find me. But remember this, Jameson. God has forgiven you your sins through Jesus Christ. He atones for us. When you know that and deeply feel that, you will be able to move on."

Jameson trudged toward his building, the reverend's last words flying through his mind. If all those years ago, he hadn't run from God but embraced Him even more, would his life have been different?

Yes!

Jameson let himself into his apartment. He made his way into his bedroom and stared at the comfort offered to him in his bed. Suddenly wide awake, he sank to his knees and bowed his head.

Thank You for sending Cassie and Reverend Rogers to

me. I think I now understand what Jesus is all about. It's Your forgiveness of my sins that will set me free.

Cassie's mother gathered her purse and walked toward the foyer. "Are you sure I can't get you anything while I'm at the store?"

Cassie shook her head, settling more comfortably into the recliner in the living room.

"I'll probably be gone about an hour." Her mom opened the front door. "Honey, call him."

"I can't," she murmured. She could still recall the expression on his face when he had left her two days ago at the hospital. While they had talked, she'd witnessed him closing himself off from her. His absence the past few days confirmed that he didn't want to have anything to do with her.

The swell of emotions almost overwhelmed her. She swallowed several times and determinedly put the man from her mind. She had to get on with her life—somehow.

When her mother left the house, Cassie stared into space, trying to make sense out of what had happened over the past weeks. Quinn Nelson had been arraigned on sports bribery and conspiracy, while Will Blake had been charged with three counts of attempted murder as well as various gambling charges. No one had yet been indicted for Scott's murder, but as she heard the evidence of the gambling scandal unfolding, she was sure Coach Nelson had silenced Scott because of the threat to his job, especially since it had come out that the assistant coach was up for a head coaching position at another school. The man hadn't been able to produce a reliable alibi for the time of her brother's murder, but there wasn't enough evidence to charge him with the crime yet.

But in the middle of all this, she felt something was missing. Someone else was involved. Neither Nelson nor Will had the intelligence to pull the point-shaving off for years. She wished she had found Scott's notebook. Maybe there were answers in there.

The doorbell drew her away from her musing. She wasn't expecting any visitors and wasn't up to seeing anyone. But when it sounded again, she rose and strode into the foyer, intending to quickly get rid of whoever it was.

When she opened the door, Jameson filled her vision, looking incredibly handsome in his usual preppy clothes. The smile that slowly transformed his serious expression stole her breath.

"May I come in?"

She stepped to the side, her heart rate speeding up.

In the living room he turned to face her. "How do you feel?"

"Why are you here?" Now she knew the wisdom in him staying away the past few days. She couldn't handle seeing him and not being important in his life.

"Can't a friend come to—"

"Don't, Jameson. Don't say another word. In the hospital you made it perfectly clear we can't be friends."

"But I didn't say that."

"You didn't have to. It was written all over your face. You couldn't wait to get away from me. So why are you really here?"

"You aren't going to make this easy for me, are you?"

"No."

He sighed. "I've been doing a lot of thinking since I last saw you. I didn't want to come see you until I was sure of what I wanted."

"And just what is that?"

"I want you in my life."

"I can't be your friend. It won't work."

He shook his head. "That's not what I want." He took the few remaining steps between them, holding up his left hand to reveal his bare ring finger. "I love you. I want much more than friendship from you."

For a moment all she could focus on were the words *I love you.* They played over and over in her mind. She hadn't realized how long she had waited to hear him declare his love until he had. Years—years of dating and finding no one lived up to Jameson.

Was she dreaming? Then her attention moved to his left ring finger, and she knew she wasn't. The gold band no longer mocked her with what couldn't be.

He wrapped one arm around her waist and gently pulled her toward him, always conscious of her bandaged shoulder. "Will you give us a chance?"

She tilted up her chin and became lost in the sky-blue of his eyes. Still stunned by his declaration, by the fact he'd finally taken off his wedding ring, she whispered, "You want to date?"

A twinkle sparkled in his gaze. "Much more than that. For years I lived in a self-imposed prison, but now I'm free. I want to spend the rest of my life with you." His mouth lifted in a grin. "But I suppose we should date for a while first." He nestled closer. "So what do you say?"

She waited several heartbeats before saying, "I love you, Dr. Jameson King. Dating is fine, but not for too long. We aren't getting any younger."

His chuckles sprinkled the air with his happiness. "Speak for yourself. I feel years younger than I have in a long time."

"But weren't you the one who told me you were too old for me?"

"What was I thinking?!" He feathered his lips across hers. "Obviously your beauty dazzled me senseless."

"Oh, that's a good recovery." She ran her fingers through his hair and brought his mouth firmly down on hers where it belonged.

* * * * *

In April 2008 don't miss the next
REUNION REVELATIONS *installment,*
IN HIS SIGHTS, by Carol Steward.

Dear Reader,

A continuity series is a writer's challenge because you work with various other authors around the country on a series of books that are connected. There are plot threads that run through everyone's stories, but at the same time your book has to stand alone. I enjoyed developing Jameson and Cassie's characters and showing how their past shaped their future. In *Don't Look Back* Jameson had to learn to let go of his past and embrace his future. Thankfully with the Lord's help, Cassie was there to show him his way.

I love hearing from readers. You can contact me at P.O. Box 2074, Tulsa, OK 74101, or visit my Web site at www.margaretdaley.com, and you can sign up for my quarterly newsletter.

Best wishes,

Margaret Daley

QUESTIONS FOR DISCUSSION

1. Cassie dealt with high school students who needed mentors. Have you ever thought about being a mentor for someone? What would you offer that person? How do you think that would change your life and that of the person you mentor?

2. Jameson was burdened with deep guilt over his wife's accident. Instead of turning to the Lord for help, he turned away when events didn't happen the way he thought they should. Have you ever turned away from God? What prompted you to seek His guidance in the end?

3. Gambling is a powerful addiction for some. It leads them down a path where they feel they have no options. In Kevin's case, in order to pay off a debt, he did something to his best friend that he lived to regret. Have you ever regretted doing something to someone? Were you able to make amends? How?

4. When Cassie was frightened and upset about going into her brother's apartment, she recited the twenty-third Psalm, which I think is very powerful. Do you have a verse you recite when troubled? Why did you choose that one?

5. What was your favorite scene in the book? What about it did you enjoy?

6. Christiana felt smothered by her older brother, who was her guardian. She wanted some independence, and he had a hard time giving that to her. Raising teens is difficult. Do you remember rebelling against your parents? Do you deal with rebellious teens now? How do you cope with the situation?

7. Jameson felt a compelling need to protect Cassie, and when he couldn't, he blamed himself for her injuries. He turned away from her because it brought back memories of watching his wife slowly fade away. He couldn't risk putting himself in that position again. Risks can be scary. Have you ever taken one that you've regretted? Have you taken one that you were glad you embraced? How would your life be different if you hadn't?

8. Did you identify with one of the characters? Which one? How?

9. Cassie came back home to take care of her mother when she was sick. Have you had to take care of a loved one because of a prolonged illness? How did your life change because of it? What helped you cope?

10. When he was hurting, Jameson withdrew into himself rather than seeking others. How do you deal with pain? Has anything made you change how you work through the hurt? Who was the first person you turn to in time of need?